SAVING
LUCAS
BIGGS

SAVING LUCAS BIGGS

by Marisa de los Santos and David Teague

HARPER

An Imprint of HarperCollins*Publishers*

Library of Congress Cataloging-in-Publication Data
De los Santos, Marisa, date.
    Saving Lucas Biggs / by Marisa de los Santos and David Teague. — First edition.
        pages   cm
    Summary: "When thirteen-year-old Margaret's father is sentenced to death for a crime he
didn't commit, she knows the only way to save him is to use the forbidden family power of time
travel"— Provided by publisher.
    ISBN 978-0-06-227462-5 (hardback)
    [1. Mystery and detective stories.   2. Time travel—Fiction.]   I. Teague, David.   II. Title.
PZ7.D339545Sav   2014   2013043189
[Fic]—dc23   CIP
                                                                                        AC

Typography by Ellice M. Lee
14 15 16 17 18   LP/RRDH   10 9 8 7 6 5 4 3 2 1
❖
First Edition

For Simon, Isaac, Michael, and Christina

CHAPTER ONE

Margaret
2014

IN THE TIME IT TOOK A MAN TO SPEAK a single
sentence, I discovered three things: there's a reason a
judge's robe looks like the Grim Reaper's; a blooming
jacaranda tree can feel like a big fat slap in the face; and
there is such a thing as a silent scream.

"For the crimes of arson and murder in the first degree,
I sentence you, John Thomas O'Malley, to death, the time
and method of which are to be determined by the Arizona
Board of Corrections."

Before Judge Biggs had finished speaking, while his
ugly words were still smashing through the courtroom, I
jerked my face away from the judge—his bat-black robe
and flat shark's eyes—and straight toward a big, arched
window.

Outside, jacaranda branches moved in the wind,

branches so thick with purple-blue flowers that it was like someone had told them, "This is your last day in all of history to bloom, so go crazy." The sight of them made me want to burst into tears, screech at the top of my lungs because, at a time like that, nothing had the right to be so beautiful and glowing and easy as those flowers against the blue, blue sky.

But I didn't cry. I sat stiller than I'd ever sat, just kind of falling in on myself, getting denser and smaller, and all the while I screamed. Not with my vocal cords, nothing so pure and ordinary as that. My mouth didn't move, but I screamed with my whole body, my hair, my fingers, the back of my neck, the pit of my stomach, the pores of my skin. I screamed until I didn't have any voice left, until I was empty, and then I floated, shivering, in an ice-cold ocean of silence.

I would have stayed there, maybe forever, but the world tugged me back. Someone's arm was around me. Someone was wailing a high, choked-throat wail (it was my mother). Someone was saying my name. And then out of all of it, my dad materialized, holding out his hands, so I went and I put my freezing hands inside them, and I'll never for my entire life forget how warm they were. But even as we stood there, holding on, he was being pulled away.

"Listen, Margaret. Look at me and listen."

I tried to do what he asked.

"Are you listening?"

I nodded.

"There is one Now . . ," he recited.

I shook my head, confused.

"Daddy."

"No. Say it. Finish the line. *There is one Now. . . ."*

I still didn't understand, but he was so insistent that I called up the rest, said the words that were as familiar as my own face in the mirror.

"The spot where I stand."

"And one way the road goes. . . ," he went on.

"Daddy! Why—?"

"And one way the road goes . . ."

He didn't let go of my hands.

I sighed and finished it, *"Onward, onward."*

> *There is one Now: the spot where I stand,*
> *And one way the road goes: onward, onward.*

The words had been passed down in our family for generations. A sort of poem. No, not a poem. A vow, a sacred one. My father called it a forswearing because it wasn't a vowing to; it was a vowing not to. When it had come my turn to take the vow, I'd done so without question. But why was he asking for it now, when there was so much else to say? What place could it have here?

His body relaxed. He kissed my hands and smiled his familiar smile at me.

"That's my girl," he said. "I love you."

"I love you, Daddy."

I said it, even though my mouth felt dry as sand. It was the best and biggest truth I had, but right then, it felt tiny and weak compared to the enormous lie that had just fallen from Judge Biggs's mouth and onto our lives like a thousand tons of bricks. For a second, my father was with me, his face the one clear thing in a world of noise and chaos.

And then—just like that—he was gone.

He didn't do it.

I know how that sounds coming from me, his daughter, his only child, but trust me when I tell you that everyone who knew him, everyone who had ever *met* him, even for a minute in the grocery line or at the gas station, knew there was no way John O'Malley could ever hurt another person. He was a fighter, yes, but a colossally kind one, the type of man who makes people—even kids—dig up words they don't usually use like "benevolent" and "gracious" and "colossally kind."

Once, when I asked how he could be so decent to everyone—because I don't find it nearly as easy—he told me it was because he figured out at some point that everyone was a human being exactly as much as he was and he had to honor that, even when it was hard.

He didn't do it. He couldn't have done it.

Ask anyone.

Even ask the jury who convicted my father. Even—and I'd bet my life on this—ask Judge Biggs with his ugly black robe and his rotten little soul who sentenced my dad to death in the same voice he probably uses to order lunch. They wouldn't admit it—no way—but deep down, they all had to know that John O'Malley could no sooner have committed that crime than he could've flown to Jupiter.

Not crime. *Crimes*.

Arson. Murder.

It would have been funny if it weren't so terrible. My father would not have burned down that stupid laboratory even if he could've gotten a signed affidavit from God that it was empty. And if he had come across it burning, just happened to be passing by, you can bet he would've run in without a second thought to save whoever might be inside.

I promise you, the words "arson" and "murder" had no business being in the same sentence with my father's name. Neither did the word "death."

Maybe I should've seen it coming. After all, he'd been convicted. If he could be convicted, if that totally wrong thing could happen, then anything could happen, right? And Judge Biggs was infamous for slapping people with the

5

very harshest sentences possible.

But more than that, the giant, towering, shameful fact was that this town, my town, Victory, Arizona, was a company town, and Judge Lucas Biggs was a company man. My dad had done about the bravest (and some would say most foolish) thing you could do in my town: he'd taken a stand against Victory Fuels.

I knew all that. But it's one thing to know facts with your mind, and it's another thing to be thirteen years old and to sit inside a courtroom in your Easter dress and watch your father, the best person in your world or maybe any, be led away in handcuffs out the door of the courtroom and out of the everyday world of freedom and sunlight and blossoming, out of *your* world, for the very last time.

Outside, the reporters waited, cawing and crowding in like a murder of crows, just like we've all seen on TV. Except that when it's happening to you, it's nothing like that because you're not watching it, you're living right inside its nightmare center, and right inside your own body, which feels stunned and stinging, like someone's been scrubbing it with steel wool, and about as exposed and fragile as a newborn kitten.

I was on the verge of total, crazy, animal panic, when my friend Charlie was suddenly right there.

"Hey," he said.

He put an arm around me, which would've been awkward in any other situation, since he and I weren't the touchy kind of friends, even though we'd known each other forever. But in this situation, it felt normal, like the first natural thing to happen all that day. As dazed as I was right then, I still felt grateful.

"Keep your head down and keep walking," he said in my ear.

I did. We followed my mom, who was being propped up by *her* best friend, Anne Jensen (or Dr. AJ), who had known me, literally, since the first second I was born, being the doctor who'd delivered me. Right before we got to the car, the reporters gave up on us and turned in unison, like a flock of idiot birds, back toward the steps of the courthouse. Roland Wise, our lawyer, was getting ready to give a statement, just like he'd told us he would.

Roland Wise was a man of his word, a lawyer who made you feel bad for ever thinking lawyers were sleazy (although I can't say the same for the prosecutor). I knew he would come by the house later, because he'd said he'd do that, too, to talk about "our next step," although in the state I was in, I found it hard to believe there was any step that wouldn't plunge us all straight over the edge of a cliff.

Just before I got into Dr. AJ's car, in the little space of sort-of quiet after the reporters had clamored away,

Charlie leaned in and said in a low, urgent voice, "So, here's the deal, no *way* are we letting them get away with this."

What he said barely registered. He took my arm and shook it.

"Hey! This is not over. Do you hear me?"

I looked blankly down at my shoes, cream-colored ballerina flats that I'd loved when I bought them, but that now seemed to belong to another girl, someone I didn't know. Same with my feet, my ankles, the hands that dangled down useless against my blue dress. None of it looked like mine.

"Margaret!"

My head felt so heavy as I lifted it to meet his eyes. Charlie, looking way too tidy. He'd gotten his always-shaggy hair cut at the start of the trial, a gesture that had made my mom put her hand on his cheek, call him "sweet boy," and cry.

"Okay," I said in some other girl's voice.

"No, seriously!" said Charlie. "Grandpa Joshua thinks he knows a way we can fix this and save your dad."

I looked over Charlie's shoulder and saw his grandfather, tall, straight, and skinny in his suit, with hair as all over the place as Charlie's usually was, but white. Same smart, serious brown eyes as Charlie's. He nodded at me, and, in a vague, disconnected way, I felt sorry for the old man for thinking that justice was possible, for thinking for a second that anyone or anything could be saved.

"Come over tomorrow morning," said Charlie, "and we'll make a plan."

His voice was so charged up, it sounded almost angry. I shook my head.

"Hey!" He gripped my arm harder.

Pulling myself away, I got into the car and didn't even flick my eyes toward Charlie until he banged on the window with his palm.

"Be there," he said.

I didn't answer, just flicked my eyes away again, staring straight ahead and not looking back, even when I heard Charlie shouting my name, over and over, fainter and fainter. Pretty soon, his voice was as gone as everything else, and I was back on that ocean of silence, as alone as I had ever been in my life.

CHAPTER TWO

Josh
1938

"NEXT STOP, VICTORY, ARIZONA!" hollered the conductor of the streamlined, high-speed, silver-sided, all-steel, superdeluxe, ultramodern Desert Zephyr. I craned my neck to see over my little brother Preston's bobbing head, but all I glimpsed was an endless range of sawtooth mountains reclining beneath a towering sky.

Two days before, a doctor in Memphis, Tennessee, had looked at an X-ray of Preston's lungs and told my mom and dad, "Take him someplace dry and sunny."

"When?" asked my father.

"Now," said the doctor.

"For how long?" asked my mother.

"Until he's well," said the doctor.

"Or . . . ?" began my dad.

The doctor just shook his head. He wasn't big on small

talk, but he had Preston's best interests at heart.

Numb, we had trudged out the door and caught a ride to our hometown, Low Ridge, Mississippi, on the back of the mail truck. With us rode a bale of Memphis newspapers. I was the one who spotted the *V* in the bottom corner of the classifieds on the back page. "Live in Victory! Work for Victory! Enjoy the good life!" read the ad. Turned out there was a coal mine in a town called "Victory, Arizona," in need of miners.

"Arizona is dry and sunny. And with a name like 'Victory,'" declared my dad, "it's the *only* place for us. Hannah! Preston! What do you——"

But my mother, reading over my shoulder, just said, "The sooner the better."

Dad telegraphed the Victory Fuels Corporation, landed one of those great jobs, raided what was left of his bankroll after the doctor visit, and bought four tickets for the Zephyr. Before I had a chance to tell the mayor of Low Ridge I wouldn't be mowing his lawn anymore, I found myself watching the sun set on a strange serrated countryside outside the window of the train while Preston's head nodded sleepily against my shoulder.

"I know," said my dad from across the aisle, studying the bemused expression on my face through narrowed eyes. "This all happened in a hurry, didn't it?"

"It's just that——I don't know anything about the desert,

Dad," I replied. "Except—in Bible stories, God is always banishing people to it when he gets mad. For up to forty years. And sometimes he afflicts them with boils. And I read that sidewinders and Gila monsters live in the prickly pear, and scorpions nest in your shoes while you sleep."

"Nobody told me about the scorpions," said my dad, shuddering.

"But 'Victory' *is* a heck of a lot better name for a town than 'Low Ridge.'"

"Much better," agreed my dad.

"And if it's good for Preston," I added, "I'm all for it."

The rhythm of the train wheels on the track began to slow, and before I knew it, we were gliding into the station. Preston woke up. "Are we there?" he asked. He reached for my hand, because he was still halfway asleep, and in his sleep, he liked me.

"We're here, Presto," I replied.

Three minutes later, the train was gone and all four of us stood rooted to our spots, staring up at a fifty-foot-high, fire-engine-red *V* looming against a sky so blue, I wanted to pour it into glasses for my family to drink.

V for Victory, the town, and *V* for the Victory Fuels Corporation.

"It's beautiful," murmured my mother. She wasn't talking about the sign, though, or even the town; she gazed at the green-shouldered mountain towering behind it all: Mount Hosta.

My dad set our bag on the platform and gawked at Victory as its lights flickered on in the dusk, absentmindedly patting his pockets for cigarettes.

"You gave up smokes two years ago, Dad," Preston reminded him.

It was true. He couldn't afford them.

My mother wobbled on the heels of her Sunday shoes and sat down suddenly on the disintegrating cardboard box held together with twine that passed for our luggage. Her hands began busily smoothing invisible wrinkles out of her best dress.

"It looks like—boats!" Preston exclaimed. "It smells like—perfume! It feels like—Thanksgiving!"

I didn't always understand what Preston was talking about. Neither did Preston. He was only nine, and his thoughts followed their own rules. Still, I got what he meant about Thanksgiving. Even though it was barely September, the breeze flowing off the high slopes behind Victory felt as crisp as November in Mississippi. I saw what he meant about boats, too. The houses of Victory reminded me of a nautical painting that used to hang in our elementary school: they glistened in rows like the fleet of ships, only the ships rode a dark wave and the houses rode a mountain.

"One of those houses is ours!" declared my father. He reached down to help Mom up, and then he hefted our alleged suitcase. Mom drew a deep breath and smiled, and when she took his trembling hand in hers, I realized they were both as nervous as I was.

As we walked down Main Street, we saw a redbrick building three stories tall. "Look at that!" exclaimed Dad. "A clock, right in the tower of the Victory courthouse." He sounded so proud, you'd have thought he put it there himself.

"There's a bank," hollered Preston. "To put all our money in!"

"And here," said my mom, "is a doctor's office: Peter O'Malley. I bet he's good. He sounds good. Doesn't he sound like a good doctor?"

"Indeed he does," replied my dad.

"A restaurant," I sang out. It was called the Globe, according to the gold letters on the plate-glass window facing the street; it featured white tablecloths and a waiter in a tuxedo. "Like in New York. Or Paris."

Inside the Globe, a family sat at a table in a pool of yellow light that flowed across the carpet and poured onto the sidewalk. The father hoisted a glass of butter-colored wine as if toasting their good fortune. The mother dangled her fork above a glistening plate of lettuce. And the two kids laughed at something she'd said. Each one had a hamburger as big as a catcher's mitt on his plate.

"Hey!" observed Preston indignantly. "They haven't taken a single bite, and the waiter is already bringing pie."

"Let's eat here, Dad," I said. When I saw his eyes widen, I quickly added, "I mean—another time—after we save up enough money. Our whole family. We'll sit at that table while the sun sets and it'll get dark outside, but we'll be together, inside, in the light."

"That," said my dad, smiling at the thought, "is *exactly* what we'll do." Then he stopped at a side street that veered straight up the foot of the mountain. "'C Street,'" he said, reading the sign.

Preston took off like an antelope. "Yahoo!" he caterwauled, flashing his sharp white teeth in the dark ahead of us.

"Preston hasn't coughed since we got here, Frederic," said my mother as we began climbing.

We passed a house with a sign in front that said SYLVIA TASSO, PIANO INSTRUCTION, which Preston eyed with distrust, because while he was big on the piano, he wasn't much for piano teachers. Dad announced, "Here it is!" stopping in front of a little bungalow perched on a level spot on the apron of the mountain. "Our new home!"

It was a real ripsnorter. Better than anything we'd ever had back in Mississippi, because there we'd lived in a lean-to made of rusty tin. The house at 403 C Street had a wooden floor, a stove, running water, a sink for washing dishes, and electric lights. It had a bedroom for my parents and one for Preston and me. It had a bathtub. *Inside* the house! The icebox was already filled with ice. My dad said somebody from the Victory company must have gathered it earlier that day in the peaks of the mountains above us and brought it down. There were fresh eggs in the icebox, too, which was good, since we were starving and all we had were the ragged socks in our lopsided box and the clothes on our backs. There was even a pine table with four chairs around it waiting for us in the kitchen.

"The company is giving all this—to us?" marveled my mother.

"They take care of their own! Three cheers for Victory Fuels!" exclaimed my dad, seating himself proudly at the head of the table like the newly crowned king of a small but significant nation.

"Look at this!" cried my mom, opening a glittering chrome bread box on the counter by the sink. "Store-bought bread!"

I cringed as Preston tore open the bag, snatched the heel, and stuffed it into his mouth, which he could stretch so wide it still gave me a start, even though I'd known him nine solid years.

We heard our new neighbor begin the Minuet in G Major by J. S. Bach on her piano.

"Tomorrow, I start work in the coal mine," declared my dad, rising from the table and taking my mother's hand. "But tonight, I hope you'll dance with me."

Preston looked at me and I looked at Preston as our parents whirled around the floor. "They're good," he admitted in surprise. "Even Dad."

"The Fred Astaire and Ginger Rogers of Arizona," I declared. We'd never known our parents had it in them.

Later, I woke up in the dark beside Preston in our new bed. He breathed as serenely as a puppy. I lay in our room, which smelled of green wood and fresh paint, watching the window curtains billow around me as if I were suspended in a cloud. The face of the old windup alarm clock I'd brought from Mississippi glowed twenty to five. A coyote sang outside. His pals joined him. Chilly desert air rolled down the mountain and poured into my room. I'd never heard a coyote in my life, and now a whole choir of them howled at the moon thirty feet from my head.

I'd never seen a mountain, and now I lived at the foot of one.

I'd never smelled the desert—and Preston was right. It did smell like perfume. Very interesting perfume. Kind of a cross between a bed of roses and an asphalt parking lot.

And Preston could breathe! I felt the dark spirit that

had been hovering over our family ever since we'd walked out of Governor's Hospital rise on the wind, turn west, and fly away.

A light appeared in the kitchen. Past my half-opened door, down the hall, I saw Dad take a seat at the table, alone in a bright yellow pool. Mom bustled up and set down an empty plate in front of him, which he stared at as if he'd never seen a plate before. Mom disappeared, but, a few seconds later, she reappeared with scrambled eggs. Before long, she was back with sausage, then coffee. Dad hardly moved. While Mom stood beside him admiring the breakfast she'd prepared, he finally picked up his fork as if to dig in, but as soon as she turned her back, he put it down and sat very still.

At five a.m., he'd start in the Victory Mine. He wouldn't come up until five p.m. For most people, that might seem like a long time, but he used to work twenty-four hours straight sometimes in Low Ridge, farming land that belonged to somebody else to raise cotton that he had to trade away for less than what it cost to feed us. Sharecropping. Sometimes the temperature hit 107 degrees. Sometimes swarms of snakes invaded the fields. But he never complained, or missed a day, and he sure as heck never got the look in his eye that he had now.

But of course he had never ridden an elevator down a hole in the ground for half a mile to spend twelve hours without seeing the sky.

"Preston still hasn't coughed," I heard my mother say. "Not once. We did the right thing, Frederic."

I reached out and found Preston's hand as he slept, and my father, because he had to, stood up straight, took a breath, squared his shoulders, kissed my mom, and clomped out into the darkness wearing new leather boots—the company had given him those, too, along with the pick and shovel leaning against our mailbox and the lamp screwed to the front of his helmet.

Peering under the edge of my bedroom curtain, I watched him trudge toward the Victory sign at the mouth of the pit.

Out of the dimness, a tall man appeared. His shoulders were approximately as wide as a pool table; he had long legs, a little bowed, turned-in toes, and enough curly black hair for a flock of sparrows to nest in. In the glow of the Victory sign I saw him laugh, snatch the helmet off Dad's head, and drop-kick it into the crowd of miners who'd materialized from the streets all around him. After the miners had played a quick soccer game with it, its shiny yellow paint looked five years old.

"Now you look like a real min-a," shouted the black-haired man gleefully, placing the helmet back on Dad's head like a bishop crowning a prince. Dad laughed. Draping his arm around my father, the man said, "Don' worry. We gonna take fine care a you!" And with that, they all stepped into the elevator and disappeared into the earth, leaving the rest of us behind in the glow of dawn.

Before Preston and I left for school, I looked up from the breakfast table to see a man standing in our kitchen. He wore expensive clothes and a smile that fooled nobody.

"How'd you get in here?" Preston asked him.

"Allow me to introduce myself," purred the well-dressed intruder. "Elijah Biggs. Manager of Victory Mine. I used to live in this very house. But I improved myself. Quite a lot. In fact, just last month, Mr. Theodore Ratliff came all the way from New York and promoted me to chief of mining operations." With that, Elijah Biggs adjusted his yellow straw boating hat, shot the cuffs of his snow-white suit, and made sure his powder-blue bow tie was riding straight.

"When Mr. Theodore Ratliff came from New York," said Preston, "and promoted you to chief . . . ?"

Elijah Biggs gazed at my little brother with mild interest. I shot a warning glance at Preston, but there was no shutting him up.

". . . did you wear that costume?" finished Preston.

"I merely wanted to extend the company's warmest greetings," said Elijah Biggs to my mother as if Preston didn't exist.

"Do you make a habit of waltzing into people's homes without—" began Mom.

"I didn't waltz," corrected Elijah Biggs. "I came to discuss your ledger."

"Our ledger?" asked Mom dubiously.

"Do you know what a *ledger* is?" asked Elijah Biggs, as if he were a kindergarten teacher and she were a five-year-old learning big words.

"Of *course* I know what a ledger is," snapped Mother.

"She went to college for three whole years," Preston cheerfully informed Elijah Biggs, "which I bet is three more than you did."

Biggs tried to pretend he didn't hear this, but I saw his eyelid twitch, which said to me that Preston probably was right.

"What I *don't* know is why the chief of the Victory Mine is in my kitchen *talking* about a ledger," continued my mom.

"This *ledger*," said Elijah Biggs, producing a black leather notebook from inside his circus clothes, "tells us your husband gets paid today when he comes out of the mine. He's new. So he won't send out much coal. But he seems like a fast learner. Let's say he'll earn twenty-five whole dollars. Which he will be paid in genuine Victory Fuels Corporation scrip." Elijah Biggs dug a crumpled piece of paper out of his pocket that looked like something cooked up by a four-year-old with a fistful of construction paper and a box of Crayola crayons. "Seventy-Five Cents," it read. "The Victory Fuels Corporation. Redeemable by Issuer Only."

"We don't get real money?" asked my mother.

"This *is* real money." Elijah Biggs smiled. "You can spend it right down the street at the company store. Where, by the way, you already owe seventy dollars."

"For what?" gasped Mom.

"Let's check the *ledger*," said Elijah Biggs, helpfully waving it in the air so we could connect the word to its meaning. "Eggs, bread, ice for the icebox, a mining helmet, lamp, pick, shovel, boots, miscellaneous furnishings, including your kitchen table—"

"But all that was waiting in our house for us!" protested my mother.

"You didn't think you got to use it without paying for it, did you?" responded Elijah Biggs. "That certainly would've been stupid, especially for someone who went to college. For three whole years."

"Frederic has been in a hole in the ground for hours working himself almost to death, and we're further in debt than when he went down!" cried Mom.

"He'll be blissfully unaware of that," replied Elijah Biggs nastily, "until he emerges from the ground."

* * *

"Today we'll begin reading *The Red Pony*," said my new teacher. "By John Steinbeck."

"Today I'll begin reading *The Red Butt*," whispered a kid sitting behind me, "by Seymour Butts."

The teacher—who was young, sort of pretty, had only a tiny mustache, and was named Miss Thuringen, according to the nameplate on her desk—didn't even blink. "You want to avoid using 'butt' twice in the same joke, Woodrow," she advised. She made it sound like a rule of grammar we all should've known.

"Yeah," I said. "How about *The Red Butt* by Seymour Heine?"

The class roared. I even chuckled a little myself until I saw Woodrow glaring at me, and noticed that he was six feet tall, and had very large fists with knuckles sticking out all over them. I hadn't started a new school since I was five, and I guess I didn't remember what happens to kids who shoot their mouths off the day they arrive.

I tried to ignore him until Miss Thuringen picked up a bell from her desk and rang it. "Recess!" she called.

I immediately did what any sane guy would do: I ran out the door and hightailed it to the farthest, dustiest, windiest, most cactus-filled corner of the school yard, and I hid behind a rock.

Peeking cautiously around my rock, I saw a kid who looked just like the guy who'd stomped on my dad's helmet before work that morning stalking my way across the skittery rock shards of the school yard. Same curly black hair. Same ridiculously wide shoulders, like a door inside a flannel shirt. Same legs, same toes. Even the same voice when he shouted at me, "Hey, kid!" only he didn't have his dad's accent. He balled up his fists, running straight my way, sporting a look you might wear to spar with a grizzly bear, so I gritted my teeth and balled up my fists, too.

"No!" he said, pointing behind me. "I'm not—"

I heard a *thunk* like a watermelon falling out a second-floor window. Fireworks exploded in front of me. My head felt like it was full of bees. The rocky ground rushed up to meet my face. Turned out that *thunk*ing sound was somebody sucker punching me. Woodrow. Assisted by three of his closest friends.

Lying on the gravel, I could easily see that Woodrow and his pals wore spotless white basketball shoes. With that fresh-out-of-the-box sparkle. My guess was these sneakers meant they all had dads who were doctors, lawyers, store owners, mine managers, or something else that made them rich, so they got to spend their time enjoying activities that didn't get their shoes dirty.

In the midst of the fog circulating around my brain, I also happened to notice that the kid with black hair wore scuffed, old, hand-me-down work boots like my own. I didn't have time to think about the deeper significance of this before he pasted Woodrow so hard across the bridge of the nose that Woodrow did a half a backflip and collapsed into a little heap.

Just like that, I had a new problem on my hands. The kid with black hair sat down across Woodrow's chest with his knees on either side and proceeded to punch him over and over in the head, howling, "You can't *do* that! You can't *do* that!" Woodrow's alleged friends vamoosed.

"Stop, Luke! Please! Stop!" begged Woodrow.

I grabbed this kid Luke under the arms and hauled like a twenty-mule team. I managed to drag him off Woodrow long enough for Woodrow to scram. Once Woodrow was gone, Luke blinked, and shivered, and managed to get control of himself. He laughed a short laugh. "Score one for the good guys," he said.

"Right," I replied cautiously.

He held out his hand. "What's your name again?" he asked, smiling a wide white smile.

"Josh Garrett," I told him. "I guess you must be . . . Luke?"

"Luke Agrippa," he replied, and we shook.

And then, standing there, not moving a muscle, I stumbled.

Luke's face turned white and I heard screams from up and down the streets of Victory.

"The mine!" whispered Luke. The second he said it, a

siren wailed, and it seemed like the whole town materialized on Main Street and began a stampede toward the base of the Victory sign, where the mine's entrance huddled under the skirt of the mountain.

"Presto! Presto!" I screamed, searching for my brother as the little kids streamed out of the school. I spotted him, and breathed a sigh of relief.

"What's wrong?" I asked Luke as I took Preston's hand.

"Collapse," said Luke, as we rode on the human wave all the way to the mine entrance. "That was the jolt in the ground."

"Two down!" shouted a man holding a telephone receiver at the gate to the mine elevator as we skidded to a halt in front of him. "Achilles Alexandropoulos. Back is broke. And they say that new fella. The one that started this morning. Tried to reach Achilles while the roof was still falling. Garrett? Garrett? What?"

Luke looked at me in horror. "Your dad," he breathed.

CHAPTER THREE

Margaret
2014

I RODE HOME FROM THE COURTHOUSE in what I guess was a state of shock, my brain numb and slow, my senses dulled, my eyelids heavy as lead. It wasn't so bad really, to feel so cut off and out of it, kind of like being a turtle dozing on a rock in a terrarium. But as soon as we turned into our driveway and I saw our house, the one my dad would never be coming back to, the glass walls of my terrarium fell right down.

Once we were inside, Dr. AJ led my mom upstairs, got her to lie down, and tried to give her a pill to help her relax and sleep.

"I can't," my mom said, shaking her head. "Margaret needs me."

Dr. AJ and I exchanged a look.

"You know what would help me, Mom?" I said gently.

"If I could lie here next to you while you fell asleep. That would be perfect."

I could see my mom trying to muster up the energy to protest again, but finally, she sighed, nodded, and held out her palm for the pill.

My mom wasn't a weak woman, but we all hit our breaking points, and my mom had hit hers kind of gradually. The first cracks appeared right after my dad's arrest—little hair-thin things, hardly cracks at all—and she got more and more broken as the weeks dragged on. By the time he was convicted, she wasn't eating enough to keep a bird alive and was sleeping so little that she'd gotten to a weird place in her mind, a twitchy, broken, manic place where she cried all the time and couldn't put thoughts together right. I'd been more or less mothering her for weeks, which felt strange, but I really didn't mind. It gave me a reason to stay steady, and anyway, after all those years of her taking care of me, I guessed it was the least I could do.

She went to sleep fast after her pill, and, after a few minutes of shifty restlessness, she looked as peaceful as she had in way too long. I almost cried then, at the sight of her, because she'd have to wake up sometime and everything would still be awful, but Dr. AJ was right beside me, and I knew that if I broke down, she'd insist on staying. What I wanted more than anything was to be alone, to sit in my own pocket of space and just breathe and *feel*, feel whatever there was to feel without worrying about anyone seeing me.

Dr. AJ seemed to get it. She called Mr. Wise and asked if he could postpone his visit until the following day. She reminded me of her cell and home numbers, even though she knew I knew them as well as I knew my own, and reminded me that she was just around the corner, which I also knew, having been to her house a bazillion times, at least. Then she wrapped me in one of her good, big-woman hugs (Dr. AJ was six feet tall and hugged like a linebacker, or like I imagined linebackers hugged), and for a few seconds I just plain clung.

"You will get through this, my girl," she said. "I have no doubt of that. Just keep the faith, you hear me?"

I nodded, even though I didn't have one scrap of faith left to keep.

As soon as she left, I realized I was starving. I opened the refrigerator, which was busting at the seams with casseroles; there must have been five or six of them, foil-covered, labeled, and stacked—and these were just from today. For months, when we weren't home, people had taken to dropping food off with our neighbor Mrs. Darley, who had a key to our house and would periodically stick them in her red wagon and wheel them on over. They gave us way more than two people could ever eat, but I knew what the casseroles meant. Every dish was someone saying,

"We've got your back."

I got as far as carving out and heating up a slab of Mrs. Alexandropoulos's famous pastitsio, which is this awesome Greek lasagna, pouring myself a glass of milk, and sitting down at the kitchen table. But as I chewed the first bite, I remembered the first time I'd eaten Mrs. Alexandropoulos's pastitsio. I was six and had just gone to my first funeral. I'm not even sure whose it was. It's what people do in Victory: there's a wedding or a funeral and the whole town shows up. Anyway, I was at the lunch afterward—there's always a lunch afterward—and I was eating the pastitsio and thinking that it was the best food ever invented, and I heard what I thought was this booming laughter. It turned out to be crying. The woman's back quaked and heaved inside the black fabric of her dress. Bobby Fitzgerald, who was sitting next to me, whispered, "It's because she's a widow. Her husband is never coming home because he's dead."

With that bite of pastitsio, the rock-solid knowledge that my father was never coming home ran up and punched me in the stomach, and that was it. I dropped my fork and cried like a baby, or more like a toddler in a fit, did the whole falling down and screeching thing I'd been teetering on the edge of since the jacaranda flowers had refused to turn black and fall off their branches.

After a long time, I got up and half crawled up the stairs, using my hands the way I used to do when it was summer and I was a little kid, wrung out like a sponge from playing all day in the hot sun. Then I fell down onto my bed and into despair, where I stuck like a bug in tar.

I wasn't usually so hopeless. When I was in third grade, I discovered the word "equilibrium" in some book my parents left lying around. I happen to be a person who collects words the way other people collect rocks or Beanie Babies. I keep the words in notebooks, the black marbled kind, and keep the notebooks, years' and years' worth, stacked inside my closet.

"Equilibrium" got a page all to itself. It's really just a fancy way of saying "balance," but I loved how long and ripply it was and how it did what it meant, how that "eek" at the front was balanced out by the soft humming "um" of the end. I guess it became a kind of motto for me. I am not necessarily a balanced person by nature, but I try. When I think a bad thought, I try to balance it out with a happy one. It doesn't work all the time, but if I do say so myself, over the years, I've gotten good at it. My mom would never let me have a tattoo, but if I ever got one, it would be that one word, "equilibrium."

What happened the evening of my dad's sentencing is that I lost equilibrium. All my life boiled down to one fact: my dad was never coming home because they were going to kill him. I knew in my bones there was nothing else, no other fact or thought or feeling to offset it, no shot at equilibrium. I guess that's my version of hitting rock bottom: being so low that even your favorite word can't save you.

I just lay there on my green flowered quilt, helpless, letting everything that had happened, all those events that had driven me to this rock-bottom spot, rumble and roar through my head and over my broken heart like a freight train.

It started with my dad becoming a whistle-blower.

"Whistle-blower" is a tricky word. On its face, it means a person who uncovers secret wrongdoing in an organization and lets the public know. But depending on your point of view and your tone of voice, it can also mean either "traitor" or "hero." When it came to my dad, a lot of the people in our town subscribed to the second definition, which was great, except that none of them were people with the power to make what they wanted to have happen happen. All *those* people, the ones with power, the ones who didn't just work for but *were* Victory Fuels—including Judge Biggs—grabbed the first definition, "traitor," with two hands, like a baseball bat, and used it to beat my family down.

Before he was a whistle-blower, my dad was a geologist, and man, did he love it. He studied rocks, which might sound boring, except that our planet happens to be made of them. So he was really studying the earth, the ground under our feet, which gives us almost everything: food, water, a place to build our houses, and a nifty little thing called fossil fuel. Coal, petroleum, natural gas. It's sort of cool to think of actually, that fossil fuels are really made of fossils, mostly plant fossils; that we're all heating our houses with old swamp grass and algae and maybe the occasional dinosaur.

Anyway, fossil fuels were Victory Fuels's bread and butter—which meant they were the bread and butter of almost everyone who lived in my town, my dad included. The company had been digging or blasting or pumping up different types of fuel from under the desert for over a century, and they were always coming up with new ways to do it. The newest way was called "hydrofracking" (often just "fracking")." In a nutshell, hydrofracking (or "induced hydraulic fracturing") is the process of injecting highly pressurized, chemical-laced fluid into a rock layer far below the surface of the earth in order to make cracks in it, and then to use the cracks to get to fossil fuels that you couldn't get to before because they were so deeply buried.

My dad's job was to find the safest places to make these fractures in the earth and to keep a close eye on the whole operation because there's a risk that hydrofracking can lead to a lot of dangerous stuff, like poisonous chemicals leaking into the water that people drink and water their crops with. Which happened. And the Biggs family, who owned the company, along with some other Victory Fuels insiders, knew it had happened, but they decided to keep it a secret because they didn't want to stop hydrofracking. Unfortunately for the town of Victory and its citizens, this secret put us in grave danger. Fortunately for most of the Victory Fuels bigwigs, they didn't live in the town of Victory, so they didn't care when my dad went to them, telling them that they had to alert the town, clean up their mess, and stop the hydrofracking. Their answer? A big fat no.

So he blew the whistle and kept blowing it. He went to the newspapers, was interviewed on TV, even created a website. He got fired, of course. But that wasn't enough for Victory Fuels. My dad got death threats; someone nearly ran my mom down one night as she walked home from her bakery; our house was vandalized. I wanted to leave, to just move away, but my parents wouldn't do it. Then, one night, a Victory Fuels lab building burned down. Inside was a night watchman, Ezra Faulkner, church deacon and father of three. He died what had to be a terrible death.

All the so-called evidence led to my father, despite the fact that he was at home with my mom and me at the time of the fire, despite the fact that my dad wouldn't harm another human being for all the money in the Biggses' bank account, despite the fact that everyone who knew anything about Victory Fuels would've bet their last dollar that the company burned that building down themselves. Whether they knew the guard was in there, well, I don't even want to guess.

Roland Wise did his best, even tried to get them to switch the trial to another town or to at least get a judge other than a member of the Biggs family to preside over it, but he hit a brick wall at every turn. Of course he did. Victory Fuels had my dad right where they wanted him. What the company wanted, it got, and what it got, it kept. That was the way of the world in Victory, Arizona. They should've put it on the town seal.

Lie upon lie upon lie piled up. Fire marshals, forensic scientists, officers of the law, officers of the court, and even a few regular citizens who we'd thought were friends— they were all in the pocket or on the payroll of Victory Fuels. The company wasn't just punishing my father. It was making sure people knew that if you defied the great and powerful Victory Fuels, it would squash you like a grape.

Who could fight power like that? Lying on my bed in the dark, with the taste of that funeral casserole still in my mouth and the sound of Judge Biggs's voice saying "death" still in my ears, I knew the answer: no one, least of all me.

Coo, coo.

It was half past midnight when I heard the mourning dove on the lawn outside my window. Of course, like all the other mourning doves I'd heard outside my window in the middle of the night, this one wasn't a mourning dove at all. It was Charlie. In movies, when people imitate a birdcall to signal each other, it usually sounds so much like the real thing that it takes the audience, as well as the person being called, a few seconds to realize what's really going on. I wish I could say this was true of my and Charlie's signal, but our mourning dove calls were quite possibly the worst in the entire history of bird calling.

This time, Charlie's call didn't wake me up for the simple reason that I had never gone to sleep. It was like once I turned myself over to that black hopelessness, there was no escaping it and nothing to do but lie there and stew in it, maybe forever. Even so, when Charlie *coo-coo*ed, I went on automatic pilot, dragged myself out of bed, grabbed a hoodie off the hook on my room door, and went downstairs.

When I got outside, Charlie was already at The Octagon. We called it an octagon because it was an octagon, about ten feet across, slightly raised, and made of weather-beaten wooden boards; we called it "*The* Octagon," first letters capitalized, because it was our place. We'd discovered it when we were in kindergarten and had had lots of wild theories, many involving aliens, about how it came to be sitting in the middle of the field behind my backyard. But even later, when we realized it was the floor of an old fallen-down gazebo, we still thought of it as special, even semimagical. And ours.

By the milky light of the moon, Charlie was drawing in his sketchbook. When I sat down at the other side of The Octagon, my knees tucked under my chin, Charlie didn't look up, just said, "Hey."

"Hey." My voice was a croak.

"I'm almost finished with the flag," he said, his pencil working away.

He meant the flag of AstraZeneca, the country we'd been working on before my dad got convicted. It was something we did, make up countries together. This had started back in second grade, when we had to give a report on the country of our choice. I had chosen France and gotten an A. He had chosen Iceland and gotten a B. Charlie still maintained that this was because my mother had baked chocolate croissants for the class, including the teacher, and had brought them in when they were still warm. He might have been right.

"Iceland's traditional dish is fermented shark meat," he had pointed out. "I was doomed."

But something about the project caught our imaginations, and before long, we were making up our own countries, giving them names that weren't country names but sounded like they should have been. Granola. Acacia. Corduroy. The Pajamas. The Grocery Isles. Calpurnia, after the housekeeper in *To Kill a Mockingbird*. We were thirteen and still playing the country game, which might have been weird, but wasn't weird to us. AstraZeneca was the name of some drug company our friend Mark's dad had gone to work for on the East Coast, but now it was the name of our latest country. And Charlie was almost finished with its flag.

"Oh," I said. I couldn't really bring myself to care.

We sat without saying anything. After a few minutes, I stretched out on my back and stared at the sky. There was too much moon for stargazing, but the bats were out, little black shapes doing their crazy, flippity swoops and crisscrossings. An owl hooted, faraway and regretful. I could hear Charlie's pencil gently *swish-swish*ing against the page and knew he must be shading.

It's not unusual for Charlie or me to "mourning dove" each other for no other reason than to sit together under the dark sky without talking, but I got the distinct feeling that this time, Charlie had something to say. I was right. After a while, in a very quiet voice with just a hint of chuckle in it, Charlie said this: "Who else would make pet rock cupcakes?"

For a second, I stopped breathing. Then I shut my eyes and slipped back in time to my seventh birthday. My pastry-chef mother was away in Tucson visiting her childhood friend Marta, who had just had twins—the only birthday of mine she'd ever not been there for—so my dad made the cupcakes, and, to put it mildly, there is a reason my dad is not a pastry chef. He did his best, though, and everything seemed to be going surprisingly well. Then, for some reason, right before he took them out of the oven, the cupcakes caved in on themselves so that each one had a pit in its center. I remember gasping at the sight of them, feeling like my own center had just sunk, and saying, "There's not time to make more, is there?"

My dad didn't miss a beat. "Make more? No way, José! These are even better than I expected. We can fill up those holes with icing. The icing's everyone's favorite part, right? They'll be great!"

And probably they would've been, except that he'd done something wrong to the icing so that, by the time the kids came, it was hard as a rock.

The first kid who bit into his cupcake yelled, "Hey, there's a rock in here!"

Again, without missing a beat, my dad said, "You bet there is. You guys are in the home of a geologist, remember? What you've got in there is known as a pet rock. Everyone gets to dig theirs out and name it!"

We played with those icing rocks for the rest of the party.

I thought for a second and then said, "Who else

would put rocks in my Christmas stocking because I'd been *good*?"

"Who else would paint a baseball with phosphorescent paint so we could place catch in the dark?"

"Who else's favorite food would be lima beans?"

"Who else would lose his glasses on top of his head—at least once a week?"

"Who else would sing 'The Star-Spangled Banner' every time he washed the dishes?"

"Who else would own six T-shirts that said Rock Star?"

We went on like that, back-and-forth, a Ping-Pong match with my dad as the ball. Charlie never tried to talk me into going to his house the next day to talk to Grandpa Joshua the way I'd thought he would. But after he left, when I was up in my room again, I realized that that was what he'd been doing all along.

Now I had something to balance out the horrible, impossible, seemingly undeniable fact that my dad would be executed, and it wasn't a fact or a feeling or an ideal like justice, but my dad himself, the real, true human person. John O'Malley, the one and only. While there was John O'Malley, there was hope. How could I have ever thought anything else? While there was John O'Malley, there was a reason to fight.

* * *

The next morning, as soon as I was up, I got on my bike and rode toward Charlie's house. With the sky still pink-streaked and shining, with the two thin tires spinning under me, I was perfectly steady, not tilting to the left or right, nowhere close to falling.

Equilibrium. I breathed the word into the morning air.

I swooped left onto Charlie's long driveway, stopped, got off, leaned my bike against the usual tree, and started walking across Charlie's yard. I was full of hope, hope so desperate and electric, it buzzed inside my head and quaked inside my chest almost exactly like fear.

Grandpa Joshua had to know of a way to save my dad. He just *had to.*

I stepped onto the Garretts' porch with its sky-blue-painted boards, its wind chimes made of old silver spoons, and its white screen door, but before I could knock or yell or just barge in (my usual means of arrival), the door creaked open, and there was Mrs. Garrett putting her arms around me and planting a kiss on the top of my head like she'd done forever and ever. She didn't say anything about my dad's sentencing, thank goodness, just swiped at her eyes, marched me into the kitchen, and said, "They're out back, waiting for you.

"Take these," she said, and handed me a batch of cinnamon rolls so fresh, I could feel their warmth through the thick stoneware plate.

"My favorite," I said, even though it didn't need to be said. I had been known to eat four in one sitting. Five, even. Okay, six, but that was just the one time, and I'd regretted it for hours afterward.

"Really?" Mrs. Garrett teased, wrinkling her nose. "You like these?"

Charlie and Grandpa Joshua sat at the wooden picnic table, which was so old it was silver-gray and smooth as glass. The picnic table, in turn, sat under the oak tree, which was so old it had a personality—crotchety and protective at the same time, like a cranky grandma. It was one of the things I loved best about Charlie's house: everything seemed to have been there forever, and nothing ever changed. When Charlie and Grandpa Joshua saw me, both of them stood up. They looked so much alike with their plaid shirts and old-fashioned politeness that I came as close to laughing as I had in days.

"Hey," I said, and slid in next to Charlie on the picnic bench.

"Hey," they both said back.

All unexpectedly, I felt shy. I'd met Grandpa Joshua lots of times before, of course, at holiday dinners and stuff, and after his wife, Grandma May, died a couple of years ago, he'd come for extended visits to Charlie's house. But I realized right then, sitting across the table from him, that we'd always been together in the hustle and bustle, the laughing, goofing, and storytelling of Charlie's family and mine. We'd talked but never *talk*-talked, and I was pretty sure we were about to have one very serious conversation.

Just when the awkwardness was getting unbearable, Charlie cleared his throat and said, "So. You're probably wondering why I brought you all here today. . . ." His voice was fake-deep and fake-serious, and he made a triangular tent with his fingers like a CEO in a movie.

Grandpa Joshua and I looked at each other and shrugged.

"Not really," I said, grabbing a cinnamon roll, opening my mouth hippo wide, and taking a bite.

"Nope," said Grandpa Joshua, doing the same.

It was a good way to begin. I've found that almost everything is better when it starts with a joke and a mouthful of really great food.

But before long, Charlie and I were sitting, serious-faced and broomstick-straight, looking at Grandpa Joshua expectantly, with our hearts in our throats. At least, my heart was in my throat, stuck there and whirring like a cicada. And if I knew Charlie—and I did—his was, too. We were all set for Grandpa Joshua to unveil a grand plan to save my dad.

Instead, he told us a story, one that he introduced by saying, "Judge Biggs has it in for your dad, Margaret. Just as he's always had it in for anyone who threatens the Victory Corporation's interests. He's bad, no doubt about it."

"He's evil," I spat. "Heartless and evil through and through."

"Maybe so. I'm not so sure about *through and through*, even now, but maybe. The thing is, he wasn't always this way. As a matter of fact, he used to be one of my favorite people in the world."

My heart stopped whirring. My heart just plain stopped.

"Wait!" Charlie squawked. "You *know* him?"

"When I was your age," said Grandpa Joshua quietly, "Lucas Biggs was my best friend."

Charlie and I just stared at him.

"Are you maybe confusing him with someone else?" I asked, finally, in a small voice. What if Grandpa Joshua's memory was going? He was old, after all. If his mind was getting foggy with old age, how would he possibly help me?

But his answer was steady as a rock: "No."

"But how could somebody like Judge Biggs be friends with somebody like you?" I asked.

"The history of our town," said Grandpa Joshua, "is full of twists like that."

Charlie, who was almost never rude, especially to adults, burst out with "Oh, come on! A history lesson? We don't have time! And anyway, we all know the history of Victory. The Canvasburg Uprising, that miner—I forget his name—who sold everyone out and killed that guy, the—"

"Maybe you know *some* of the story," interrupted Grandpa Joshua, as heated up as I'd ever seen him. "Maybe you learned a *version* of it in history class. But there's more to it, so much more that you might want to reconsider everything you ever believed about Victory, Arizona."

Fine. But how in the wide world did this have anything to do with my dad? I itched with impatience, but then I happened to get a look at Grandpa Joshua's face. His usually kind brown eyes were fierce and sad and full of something I couldn't name, maybe with *his* version of history, the one he'd carried around all this time, maybe with the truth that would set my dad free. I did my best to shove my impatience away.

"Okay," I said. "Tell us. Please."

"There are a lot of ways to break a person," began Grandpa Joshua. "And Victory Fuels had a pretty good handle on all of them. People's spirits they broke in the cruelest way: by first lifting them up, by making their workers, folks who'd traveled hundreds of miles for a new life, at first believe that they'd found one. But at some point, usually pretty early on, those families, mine included, would wake up and realize that while they'd been enjoying their decent house and their three meals a day, a trap had fallen smack down around them.

"The Victory Mine broke bodies, too," he continued.

There was a tiny, sorrowful catch in his voice, and

that's when Grandpa Joshua's story stopped being a history lesson and started being a story about real people, and even though I was dying for him to get to the part in it where my dad gets saved, I knew I had to listen to every word of what came next.

CHAPTER FOUR

Josh
1938

EIGHT HOURS AFTER THE MINE collapsed, when Aristotle Agrippa and his rescue party finally carried my dad out, two of his ribs were broken and he had a fear of the dark that haunted him the rest of his life, but he was alive, and the very next day he went back to work. Mr. Alexandropoulos, whose life Dad had saved by running deeper into the shaft when he should've run the other way, was not so lucky. His backbone had cracked and he would never walk again.

So Elijah Biggs, the boss of the mine, fired him as he lay in his infirmary bed, then marched over to his house dressed in an expensive suit the color of sherbet and threw his family into the street. He even helped carry out a lamp and a few dishes.

"The Victory Corporation isn't a charity!" Biggs

informed the angry mob of miners that gathered in the yard to protest. It had already footed the bill for his infirmary stay and would probably never see that money again. And now, how could Mr. Alexandropoulos work in the mine if he was in a wheelchair? And how could he live in a Victory house if he didn't work in the mine?

The crowd rippled, eddied, and murmured in anger. The two hulking "associates" in cheap suits who accompanied Biggs everywhere stood on his right and his left glowering, daring anybody to complain. Folks turned around to slink home. Biggs smirked in triumph. But Aristotle Agrippa, strong and straight, made his way through the crowd, and as we closed ranks behind him, we stood taller, and nobody felt like retreating anymore.

When Aristotle got to the Alexandropouloses' front porch, face-to-face with Biggs, he said, "You got to stop this." Everything and everybody fell silent. Even the thugs who passed for Biggs's bodyguards put civil expressions on their flat faces to listen.

"*You,*" spluttered Biggs, "can't tell *me* to stop!"

"We can tell you what's right," replied Aristotle simply. "And what's right is, you got to stop."

Biggs turned to his stooges and muttered, "Fix this." They shuffled their feet and glanced at each other and didn't do it right away, because Aristotle stood there looking like something his forefathers in Athens might've carved from marble and set up in the town square, something you didn't necessarily want to ball up your fist and punch.

"No," said Aristotle, never taking his clear gray eyes off Biggs. "*You* take care of this."

"I just did," taunted Biggs, pointing at the Alexandropouloses' possessions in the street.

"If you gonna do this to Mrs. Alexandropoulos," Aristotle informed Biggs, "better do it to me, too."

"What?" snapped Biggs.

"I ain't gonna work for you," declared Aristotle.

"Then you just lost your house," barked Biggs.

"I know," said Aristotle.

My dad limped forward right away and said, "I quit, too."

And then and there, the whole crowd quit in protest, right down to the guy who oiled the elevator cable.

"Who—who's going to work the mine?" stammered Biggs.

"We will," answered Aristotle, "after you do what's right."

And so we found ourselves in a camp on the edge of town that became known affectionately as "Canvasburg" because of the huge old army tents from the Great War Mr. Darley's veteran friends had donated for us to live in. Across town, the Victory Mine sat empty, earning not a penny. Biggs tried hiring replacements, a bunch of unemployed farmhands from Colorado, but they had no idea what they were doing and only managed to derail the mine train, start a fire in the elevator, and flood a quarter mile of tunnel, all without bringing out a single lump of coal. Soon, word went around that Biggs was up to his eyeballs in hot water with *his* boss in New York because he was losing money so fast.

The homemade tank showed up right after this rumor started.

It wasn't much to look at. Just an old Model T with leaky tires, manhole covers welded all over like armor, and a machine gun bolted to the floor where the backseat used to be. It lumbered stupidly around the edges of our camp like an eyeless crab searching for prey at the bottom of the ocean. Biggs claimed it was manned by "detectives" protecting the upstanding people in the brick homes of Victory from us hooligans down in Canvasburg.

All the mining families met in an open spot amid the tents to decide what to do about it.

Mr. Martinelli stood up and said, "I got a hunting rifle!"

A murmur went through the crowd at the mention of a gun.

Aristotle rose slowly in the firelight, and from where I sat, he loomed even larger against the sky than the Victory *V.* Quietly, as the Model T motor coughed in the darkness and the creepy machine nosed around our camp, he said, "No guns. I seen what guns do. In the Great War."

"But *they* started it," challenged a voice from the crowd. "*They* brought the tank. *They* want to fight. It's only fair if we—"

"We gonna fight," Aristotle replied, as the whole crowd strained to catch every word. "But not like that."

"Then how?" demanded the voice. A voice I recognized. Luke's.

"There's good people out there," said Aristotle, staring across the dark desert as if he could actually see them. "I know them. We gonna tell them what's happening. They help us."

"We should give Victory a taste of their own medicine!" persisted Luke.

"Maybe, son," replied Mr. Martinelli, nodding thoughtfully at Aristotle as he sat down again, "but maybe not yet."

The next morning I heard a "pock" on the side of my family's tent. I thought Luke was out front tossing acorns for a joke. Then I noticed a brand-new hole letting in sunlight, a hole the size of a bumblebee. I saw another one just like it in the far wall. For a few seconds, Mom and Dad and I stared at the dust motes swirling through the pencil-thin sunbeam. Preston sat frozen on his piano stool. Aristotle and Luke, who had come over like they did just about every morning to give my mother wildflowers they'd found by Honey Brook, froze in their tracks. The report of a gun echoed into silence among the hills.

And for a moment, even though it had two bullet holes in it, our tent still did its best to be our home.

There was the iron stove my mother cooked on, in the corner, cooling after breakfast. There were the pictures of our grandparents on the upright piano my dad had salvaged from a boarded-up church on the far side of the mountains in Mercury, New Mexico, so Preston could practice for his teacher, Mrs. Tasso. It still rang from the last note of the last scale Preston had played.

There was the bookshelf with the collected works of Charles Dickens on it we'd scavenged from beside the curb on trash day in the brick part of town.

There was my bed. Came from the same place. And in a corner, a bicycle we'd dug out of the dump. At least it was my bicycle that day. Luke and I shared it—we each kept it twenty-four hours and then it went next door.

For a few moments, it seemed like the stove and the bicycle and the piano and the other things we'd collected to fill up our cloth home would win. It seemed like that hole had never appeared, like the gunshot had never sounded.

"What . . ." Preston held up his right hand in wonder. His eyes were wide and his mouth made a perfect O of surprise. Three of his fingers were gone.

Then the machine gunner pulled hard on his trigger and we heard the yammer of his weapon as it cut our tents to confetti.

A bullet caught my mother in the leg and toppled her.

"Down! Down! Everybody down!" shouted Aristotle, pressing Luke and me flat on the floor of our tent. "The stove!" he said to my dad, who dragged Preston to it and shoved him under and turned around and did the same with Mom. They fit, but barely.

In the meantime, Aristotle grabbed the piano and shoved it onto its face. Beneath the keyboard, he hid Luke and me from the flying bullets.

"Stay, boys," ordered Aristotle. "Josh's dad and me, we going around to hide people behind all the stoves and iceboxes."

"No!" argued Luke. "Get Mr. Martinelli's gun. We have to stop those guys!"

"Be still, Luke!" barked Aristotle. To my dad, he said, "Frederic. Let's go." I think he knew, after my dad had risked his life to save Mr. Alexandropoulos in the mine shaft, that he was brave enough to do what they were about to do.

As soon as their shadows disappeared, Luke bolted from under the piano. Outside, the gunfire had slowed to short, jumbled bursts. "Luke!" I hollered as he scuttled, head low, around the corner of the tent and headed for the

Martinellis'. He didn't listen, so I chased him. The gunshots seemed to have moved farther off.

I could hear a baby wailing and someone was shouting for her family members in panic. A thin tendril of smoke drifted up from our left, but above it all, the sunlight blazed and the air was crystal clear.

Inside her tent, Mrs. Martinelli lay on the floor, unhurt. Beneath her, protected by her bulk, lay her four kids. "Where's Mr. Martinelli?" asked Luke. "Where's his gun?"

"He took it," panted Mrs. Martinelli. "He's up in the mountains hunting for dinner!"

"For crying out loud!" shouted Luke. "What are we going to do?"

"Find something heavy," I replied, scanning the tent, "to shelter the Martinellis." Unfortunately, they didn't seem to own a stove. But they had dug a fireplace right in the middle of their floor, under a hole in the canvas roof that let smoke out. It was at least two feet deep and three feet across.

Four rounds spattered across the floor, kicking up dust and bits of gravel, followed by four burps from the machine gun. Bullets, I was learning, travel faster than the sound of the gun that fires them.

"Get in!" I shouted, surprised at how steady I sounded as I picked myself up off the floor. It occurred to me that if

I got killed, I'd never hear the shot that did me in.

But mostly I thought: *Is everybody safe?*

Mrs. Martinelli tossed her kids into their cooking pit like sacks of salt and leaped in behind them. Luke was already out the door, but when I tried to crab-walk after him, I felt a tug. Mrs. Martinelli, reaching over the lip of her hiding place, had me by the ear. "Climb in here, you little fool!" she screeched.

"No," I said. "I have to help."

Her free hand happened to land on an iron frying pan lying nearby.

"Luke's out there," I protested, frantically trying to wriggle free of her grasp before she dragged me into the pit.

Mrs. Martinelli drew her skillet back. Just as she cocked her elbow to clock me, a slug zinged off it. She dropped the frying pan like it had just come off a red-hot stove, and I made my escape, leaving her to the safety of their accidental foxhole.

Outside, I found Luke dragging Ed Kowalski toward his tent. Ed had been shot in both feet. I took one arm and Luke took the other, and we managed to get Ed inside. They say reading is good for you. Turned out, it sure was good for Ed. He and his brothers had a tin steamer trunk full of old detective novels they'd read over the years. That thing was three feet high and four feet thick and jammed solid with cheap novels. It stopped slugs better than armor plate. By now, we knew exactly where the tank was firing from—on the side of a hill due east of Canvasburg—and Luke and I hid Ed behind his books and crouched there with him.

The sound of whimpering came from nearby. "The Tiklas kids," moaned Ed. "Next door." Luke and I looked at each other. Neither of us said a word. We slithered under the wall of Ed's tent and then under the wall of the Tiklases'.

"An icebox!" shouted Luke. We pushed it over on its side and stuck the Tiklas kids behind it. A burst of fire riddled the radio by my elbow, and then the shots drifted up into the branches of a tree outside. "They're not even aiming," muttered Luke, watching the stream of gunfire wander off into the desert outside the door. "They're shooting from the hill in front of camp, but they're just taking potshots."

"Hundreds of potshots," I added.

Luke threw back his head and, at the top of his lungs, shouted to the whole camp: "They're firing from the hill to the east! Get behind something heavy! You'll be safe!"

"A stove. An icebox. A piano," I hollered.

From nearby, I heard somebody take up the call and pass it down the rows of tents. The message made its way around camp. Then silence fell.

"Luke? Everybody's safe?" I whispered.

"Maybe," said Luke cautiously.

"Help," came a voice. "Help me."

"Mrs. Tasso?" I called.

"I can't move!" she wailed. Mrs. Tasso was eighty-nine years old and frail as a sparrow.

"Her tent is three rows away," I said. As I thought about running through the open to get there, all the fear I hadn't had a chance to pay attention to before suddenly rose inside me like a black tide.

"We better go now, before they start shooting again," said Luke.

In the clear sunlight of the morning, it was plain what Luke and I had to do—and that we'd do it together.

We bolted for Mrs. Tasso's tent.

We found her crouched in the middle of her floor. "Where's Mr. Tasso?" I asked.

"He's up in the hills fishing in Honey Brook," she said.

Instead of knocking over her old piano for shelter, Luke laid hold of a giant oak cupboard and yanked it onto its face. A cascade of crockery poured out, along with a pistol. We got Mrs. Tasso hunkered down in the remains of her dinner dishes, and Luke snatched the gun and bolted.

I followed through thickening smoke and found him struggling with his father behind an old coal hopper at the edge of Canvasburg, fifty yards from where the tank sat parked and silent. Just as I got there, Aristotle took the gun.

". . . they can't do that!" Luke cried as I crab-walked up. "It's not right! We have to show them!"

"You get yourself shot, my brave Luke, and that don't help nobody!" Aristotle rejoined, restraining him.

"Come on, Luke," I chimed in. "Those aren't playground bullies! They're crazy! And they have a machine gun!"

"What should we do then?" retorted Luke. "Just hide here and take it?"

Aristotle looked at the gun in his hand with resignation in his eyes. My dad, at that moment, came scrambling up. "I think everybody's covered," he said. "I don't think they can hit anybody unless they move the tank."

Aristotle opened the chamber of the pistol. I could tell it was something he'd done before. "Empty," he said, dropping it on the ground like he was relieved to be rid of it. "Okay."

And with that, he took off running in a giant sweep toward the tank. Nobody inside seemed to notice. "They don't see him," observed my dad. "They've been firing blind this whole time. They didn't leave any way to aim when they built that ridiculous thing."

"Did Aristotle know that before he ran off?" I asked. My dad shrugged.

Luke watched, his fists clenched, shaking. I saw him wipe away a tear. "Be careful, Daddy," he whispered. "And get 'em!"

Aristotle had circled all the way around behind the tank and scaled the back. Frantically, we watched the nose of the machine gun swivel in his direction, but it couldn't turn far enough. "They can't point their gun backward," muttered my dad.

As we watched, Aristotle appeared on top. He unscrewed the hatch, reached in, and yanked out a man. The man was surprisingly scrawny, and dirty, and sheepish. "You shot first!" we heard him whine.

"With what?" demanded Aristotle. "We don't got guns." He tossed the man to the ground, and the man scuttled away.

He reached in and fished out another. "Somebody threw a rock!" this one complained.

"Hogwash!" bellowed Aristotle, and threw him off the tank to skitter after the first, smacking the dust off his hands as the guy disappeared into the brush.

"That was the bravest thing I ever saw in my life," I breathed.

"I never even saw anything close," said my dad.

"He let 'em go!" replied Luke in astonishment. "What's wrong with him? He should've pounded 'em! He should've wrung their necks! They shot at us, for Pete's sake! Is he yellow? Is he—"

"Luke," said my dad gently as Aristotle jumped down from the tank and made his way toward us. Luke stared at Dad wildly, and my father put a hand on his shoulder, holding him until he calmed down. "You and Joshua find water. Bring it to the hurt people, because they've lost a lot of blood."

"Come on, Luke. Come on," I said. Slowly, Luke followed me back to camp, where we found a tin cup and a bucket, which we took to Honey Brook.

We heard the sound of sobbing and spotted the three Rodi kids behind one of the flowerpots Mrs. Tasso had planted in the middle of camp to pretty things up. "Everything's going to be okay," said Luke quietly, even though he said it through clenched teeth, and he was shaking with rage.

Down the way, I saw my dad give me a thumbs-up from our tent. Preston and my mom were alive.

"We should check on Mrs. Tasso again," I said. We ran to her tent. In front lay Mr. Tasso. Two trout had fallen out of his creel, and they twitched in the dust as their gills worked uselessly. Over him knelt Mrs. Tasso.

"He's dead," she gasped, looking into my eyes. "Joshua! My Theophilus is dead!"

"I'm sorry," I said. I didn't know what else to say, or to do. I saw that she was wounded, too, her dress sopping with blood, and I remembered what my dad had said. "You should take a drink," I told her. But I'd spilled all our water. "Wait, Mrs. Tasso," I said. "I'll be back."

Luke sat beside her while I ran. I filled my bucket, but I didn't go back right away. I was too sad, I was too afraid, I was too confused. When I came back, Mrs. Tasso had died. Luke still held her hand.

"Mrs. Martinelli!" I cried, spotting the smoldering ashes where her tent used to be.

They were all dead. Mrs. Martinelli and her children. The gunfire hadn't so much as grazed them. They'd stayed safe in the pit in the middle of their tent. But one of the last bullets to fly had shattered her kerosene lamp, and it had set their tent aflame, and the fire had left nothing for them to breathe in their hideout. The whole thing had happened in seconds. Mr. Martinelli ran down the mountain when he heard the gunfire, but he was too late.

Doc O'Malley came. He was from town, but it turned out he wasn't one of *them*. Everybody who wasn't dead, he saved. He didn't say a whole lot. He didn't have a nurse, a partner, or an assistant. He just worked and worked, stitched and palpated, examined and scrutinized with his blazing green eyes, set bones and observed and listened and kept Luke and me running back and forth to the pharmacy for hours straight, scribbling down orders on a prescription pad, handing them over without looking up from Sally Tiklas or my mother or my little brother. And Joe Donahue, the pharmacist, stayed up all night and filled every one, handing each bottle back to Luke or me without saying a word about money. Mr. Donahue was a terrible businessman but a great human being.

Later, in the dark, on the edge of Canvasburg farthest from the mountain, hidden from the lights of Victory, Aristotle and my dad and Luke and I dug graves. Four small ones. Plus three the size of grown-ups. Others from Canvasburg pitched in to help: Mr. Darley, the Rubino sisters, and all three patched-up Kowalski boys. When the sun rose on the far side of the plain, the graves were done. At sunset that day, we held the funerals.

There wasn't a preacher, so Aristotle stood under a cottonwood tree by Honey Brook and said as much as he could say. And what he said was: we were going to stay. All of us. We would never leave those children where they lay, or their mother, or Mr. or Mrs. Tasso, because we loved them. We would keep living our lives right here.

Mr. Martinelli, who'd been staring into the sky like he was hypnotized, shouted, "I'm going to kill them! Every one of them! I'm going to take my gun and find them and kill them, starting with Biggs! I'm declaring war on the Victory Corporation!"

We all looked at Aristotle. Especially Luke.

And Aristotle said it again. "We gonna do better than that for these souls, our friends. We gonna take away the occasion of all wars."

"What are you talking about?" demanded Mr. Martinelli.

"Nobody out there even knows what's happening to us. We're on our own. We need guns. We need to fight."

"Look," Aristotle said, unfurling a sheaf of paper he'd stowed in his jacket. "I been writing letters. To people I know. Good people. This guy, Walter Mendenhall, he's a reporter, he writes for the *Weekly World Worker*, in Denver, Colorado, he gonna tell people. They gonna be out*raged!*" And for a second, I could see it. Deep in Aristotle, under his bravery and his calm, he was as angry as any of us. But he held it tight and kept it buried deep.

"*If* he agrees to write about our story," my mother added, leaning forward in the kitchen chair we'd set out on the grass for her. "And *if* anybody bothers to read the *Weekly World Worker*. That's a radical paper, Aristotle. It's not exactly the *New York Times*."

"We gonna get him to write about us," said Aristotle. "And people gonna read about us." And really, the way he said it, I had to believe him, and I guess everybody else did, too, even Mr. Martinelli, who dropped his eyes to the ground and fell silent.

Everybody except Luke. "We need to *fight*, Dad!" he protested. "For *ourselves!*"

"That's what we're doing, my Luke," said Aristotle.

But Luke just turned away in disgust.

CHAPTER FIVE

Margaret
2014

I SWEAR I DIDN'T STOP THINKING about my dad the whole time Grandpa Joshua told this story, never stopped seeing his beautiful green eyes behind his glasses or the handcuffs chafing his wrists as he walked away from me in the courtroom, but I couldn't keep from getting sucked right into Grandpa Joshua's tale, which wasn't just his but mine, too. Because a place isn't just a snapshot of itself in the present; a place is everything that ever happened in it. I listened and realized that I'd lived in Victory my whole life without ever really knowing where I was.

And for a few minutes, anyway, Grandpa Joshua's story took a turn for the brighter, veered away from gunfire and broken families, straight toward peaceful negotiation and hard-won, good, solid change.

Because the letters written by Aristotle and the miners

began to work! Folks across the country began making noise. Outraged noise. Clamoring-for-justice noise. The noise traveled all the way to New York City, straight through the thick stone walls of Victory Fuels's owner Theodore Ratliff's palatial mansion, into the ears of Ratliff himself, and even though those ears were probably more used to opera, Beethoven, and flattery, they listened. Ratliff agreed to give the miners what they asked for.

"Which wasn't that much, when you think about it," I said.

"Basic, ordinary American stuff," said Charlie. "A safe place to work, a fair salary, 'life, liberty, and the pursuit of happiness.'"

Grandpa Joshua smiled at us with pride in his eyes. Then he said in a tired voice, "We came so close."

"What happened?" I asked.

"We know what happened. Or some twisted version of it," said Charlie, bitterly.

I'd gotten so caught up in hearing the story of Canvasburg, that I'd almost forgotten I'd already read about it in our school history book.

"Oh. Right," I said, struggling to recall. "The meeting in the cigar parlor of Ratliff's hunting lodge to sign the miners' new deal. Mr. Ratliff, Aristotle Agrippa, and Elijah Biggs. Three people went in, two came out. That's what the book said. 'Three went in, two came out.' And

Theodore Ratliff stayed where he was, stabbed to death on the parlor floor, murdered by Aristotle."

I slapped the table in realization. "But he didn't! He wouldn't!"

"No way!" said Charlie.

"No," said Grandpa Joshua. "And Aristotle was nearly half dead himself, he'd been bashed over the head so hard. Again, it was Doc O'Malley who stepped in; saved his life, Doc did. But while Doc was busy doing what he did best, so was Biggs. Before he set foot out of that hunting lodge, the man was spreading lies. He claimed that Ratliff tricked Aristotle, went back on all his promises to improve life for the miners, and tried to force Aristotle to go back and make the miners return to work anyway. Biggs said that was when Aristotle chickened out, said he couldn't face the angry miners, and asked for money to get out of town right then and there, that same night. When Ratliff laughed in his face, Aristotle went into a rage and killed him. Biggs launched a full-out smear campaign, calling Aristotle a traitor, a coward, and a liar to anyone who would listen. Including, I'm sorry to say, Luke."

"But he didn't listen, did he?" Charlie said.

Grandpa Joshua rubbed his forehead.

"Biggs tailor-made his lies just for Luke, worded them perfectly, and the man was a champion liar. Besides, Luke was just a kid, and he was already down on his dad for refusing to fight, so, well, I'm afraid the lies started to work."

Almost in unison, and in the same stunned tone, Charlie and I said, "What?"

How could anyone not stick by his own father, especially a father as brave and noble as Aristotle? I thought of my own dad, locked in a cell, and hot tears filled my eyes. I'd cut off my own arm before I'd turn on him.

Grandpa Joshua sighed.

"Luke Agrippa was a good kid. He loved his dad. But despite being better-looking and a better athlete than anyone around, he couldn't stand the idea of being seen as weak or cowardly. He even came up with a plan to steal some guns, arm all of us, and fight back, but Aristotle squelched it. Truth is, Luke had kind of despised his dad ever since the massacre. But I know he would've rallied and stood by Aristotle in the end if it hadn't been for the terrible thing that happened next."

I tried to remember what we'd learned in school, but it was hazy.

Charlie jumped in. "Aristotle committed suicide before he was tried for Theodore Ratliff's murder, and Elijah Biggs, the new president of Victory Fuels, restored order. That's all I remember."

"But I don't believe Aristotle would've killed himself!" I cried. "No father would do that, knowing his kid was out there, waiting for him to be set free and for everything to go back to normal!"

"He wouldn't have, and he didn't," said Grandpa Joshua. "No matter what the history books say, I know that like I know my own name. Biggs and his henchman were just finishing off what they'd started in the hunting lodge. They were smart enough to know Aristotle would never stop fighting for the miners, not even from prison. So they got rid of him. They must've dragged him out of his bed in the town infirmary and hanged him by his bedsheets from a beam in front of one of the windows, because that's where he was found."

I felt like someone had punched me in the stomach.

"Aw, man," breathed Charlie.

"It was a pitiful, horrible, low-down thing," said Grandpa Joshua quietly. "And oh, what it did to Luke."

"He was angry? Sad?" I asked.

"Worse. I was by Luke's side when he joined the crowd gathered around his father's poor body. Inside, he must have felt a thousand things, but what he looked was ashamed. Sick with shame to be his father's son and ashamed to be ashamed. The boy was just ruined. After that, Biggs and the company dive-bombed him like the vultures they were and swept him up. He was lost. I tried to talk to him, to stop it, but he turned on me, too. The Luke I knew, my best friend, was gone for good the second he saw his father's broken body swinging from that beam. Somehow, he set his mind on believing the worst about his dad, and that's exactly what he did from that day forward. Before I knew it, even before they changed his name officially to Biggs, he was one of them."

Charlie and I should have seen this coming, but we'd gotten so caught up in the story that we hadn't. We gaped at each other in horror and amazement.

"Luke Agrippa became *Judge Lucas Biggs*?" I could barely choke out the words. My head was spinning so hard that I didn't even fully understand what I was thinking until Charlie spoke.

"They killed his father for a crime he didn't commit, and now he's going to help them do the same thing to Margaret's dad?"

"Luke spent his life believing his father was a loser, a coward who killed himself," said Grandpa Joshua simply. "And once Luke was all alone in the world, Biggs gave him everything: a home, some fancy boarding school, college in France, Harvard for law school. Made him feel strong and powerful, like he'd always wanted. The Biggs family and Victory Fuels own him as sure as they own all that hydrofracking equipment. I think they have ever since the day his father was murdered," said Grandpa Joshua.

"If only——" I said and stopped, shivering in the warm sunlight.

I gazed up at the sky and thought about how somewhere up there, under all that blue, the stars were burning, were arranging themselves into patterns.

Grandpa Joshua leaned toward me, his eyes bright.

"If only what, Margaret?" he asked in this odd voice, calm but sharp as a knife.

I shook my head. "There's no use thinking about 'if only.'"

"Maybe there is," said Grandpa Joshua. "What were you going to say?"

His face was so focused and intense, it almost scared me. His eyes never left mine.

I shrugged. "If only someone could've been there to stop what happened in that hunting lodge," I said.

"Yeah," said Charlie, catching on. "If there had never been a murder for Luke's father to get accused of, if someone had stopped it, then maybe Luke would never have gone down the road he went down."

I didn't want to continue that conversation, but somehow I couldn't help myself. "And maybe he wouldn't have turned out the way he has, and maybe my father wouldn't have just been sentenced to death."

Grandpa Joshua leaned toward me across the table. My breath came quicker. *He knows*, I thought, which was crazy. He couldn't have known. No one knew.

"If only someone could *go back in time*," said Grandpa

Joshua in the same strange voice, "if only someone could go back and save Theodore Ratliff, they would also save Aristotle, and save Luke, and save your dad, too, Margaret."

He knew. I didn't know how, but somehow he did.

I leaped to my feet so fast, I knocked over my glass.

"No!" I said. "I can't. History doesn't want to change. History resists! And I promised I wouldn't. We all promise."

"What?" asked Charlie, alarmed. "What are you talking about?"

> "There is one Now: the spot where I stand,
> And one way the road goes: onward, onward."

Because I was thinking the words in my own head, because the words were a secret from everyone but my family, because no one else could possibly know them, much less speak them out loud, it took me a second to realize that that was exactly what Grandpa Joshua was doing.

"No," I whispered, backing away. "You can't know about the forswearing. You can't."

"When I was your age," Grandpa Joshua said gently, "I met a woman who was decades older than I was, but who would become my lifelong friend. She sent me to college, helped me get out of this town, and got my little brother out of it, too. She was like a grandmother to me, but she would've been your great-great-aunt."

I tried to make sense of what he was saying, but my pulse was pounding in my ears.

"One day," he went on, "not long after I met her, she told me a story about her family and the promise they all made, and about herself and how she was the one who broke it."

"Grandpa! Don't you see that you're scaring her? What is all this about?" cried Charlie.

"Margaret," said Grandpa Joshua. His clear voice was hushed, but it seemed to ring out over the yard. "Your father is a good man and an innocent one."

A sob broke from my throat.

"What the heck is going on?" said Charlie.

I wrapped my arms around myself and felt the earth tilting under me; Grandpa Joshua's story, my father's face, the words of the forswearing, the stars moving invisibly in the blue sky, all spiraling like a hurricane inside my head, and then I turned and ran across the yard as fast as I could run.

CHAPTER SIX

Josh
1938

AFTER THE MASSACRE, OUR JOB was to keep Canvasburg alive, because if we left, or starved, or froze in the fall wind that'd started cascading down Mount Hosta, everything that'd happened to us would disappear into thin air, and everybody who'd died would've died for nothing.

Mr. Martinelli stopped talking about going after the Victory Corporation with guns, and a huge sadness descended over him. He didn't speak for days at a time. But when our food began to run out a few weeks later because we weren't allowed in the company store, and even if we had been, nobody had any money anyway, he went tent to tent with a canvas bag collecting up every spare tin of sardines, every box of cracker crumbs, every dented can of Campbell's soup, and he set up an iron pot over a tumbleweed fire on the ground, and somehow, three nights a week, he boiled all this into enough stew to feed everybody.

Of course, that left four nights of nothing. And we got hungry. And we got cold.

So we wrote letters to give ourselves a purpose.

Aristotle sent the Kowalski brothers on a mission to the nearest library, three towns away through the mountains, to fill up a notebook with the names and addresses of reporters, politicians, preachers, writers, singers, movie stars, doctors, lawyers, baseball players, you name it, people from all over the country—anybody who might care about what'd happened to us.

Then we began putting down our story on paper and mailing it all over the country. Aristotle wrote more than anybody. He had a giant black fountain pen carved of ebony that his grandfather had given him to do his schoolwork with when he was a little boy in Greece. He scrawled out whole bales of letters. He must've used half a gallon of ink a week, even though he was awfully weak on spelling, commas, and putting *s*'s on the ends of verbs. My mother helped him out as much as she could with his English, but there was nothing she could do about his handwriting, which gave the impression a centipede had fallen in an inkwell, swum across, climbed out, and swarmed across his page. Still, Aristotle's letters were masterpieces, sometimes ten pages long, telling the story of who we were and what had happened to us, so people put up with the penmanship.

We wrote to President Roosevelt. We wrote to Eleanor. We wrote to Babe Ruth, and we even sent a letter to a guy named Woody Guthrie, some new singer a few people had heard about. And after the day's letters were written, Aristotle crept out of camp and sneaked through the mountains in the dark to Mercury, thirteen miles away, to mail them, dodging the Victory company's so-called detectives, who had guns and strict orders not to let us communicate with the outside world. He always made Luke stay behind, no matter how much Luke begged. We invited Luke to sleep in our tent while Aristotle was gone, but he was too proud to admit he was lonely, so he never did.

Fall kept falling, and the desert nights grew colder. I got to thinking that if we stacked rocks around the edges of our tents to stop the mountain wind from whistling straight through, then maybe our blankets wouldn't blow off in the middle of the night while we tried to sleep, leaving us dreaming of glaciers and hugging our knees. What I didn't foresee was how hard it would actually be to find a rock to pick up. Even *one*. I mean, the desert around there, the whole shimmering thing, was like a work of art. It should've had a guard in a uniform and a sign: Do Not Touch.

It was perfect. It was beautiful. Red! Green! Yellow! Blue!

Brighter than you ever imagined! Every rock fit into every other rock like the pieces of a mosaic.

When I finally did locate a loose stone that didn't look like it'd mind being picked up, it turned out to have the outline of a leaf embedded in it.

"Petrified fern," observed Luke from behind me.

I dropped the fern on my foot. "I thought you had football practice," I said, hopping around like a Ringling Brothers clown. Even though almost nobody on the football team was actually speaking to him, because they were all Victory kids, Luke still got to put on his helmet and his pads and play quarterback, son of a Greek miner or not, since there was nobody else in Victory who could throw a fifty-yard pass, and without a quarterback, how were they going to beat Mercury, New Mexico?

"I don't need to practice," he said. "Coach says I couldn't be much better than I already am."

If another guy had said this, he might've sounded like a lunk, but Luke just sounded like he was telling it like it was, because he was.

"I was looking for something to weigh down the corners of our tent," I told him, "but——"

"It kind of feels like robbing a church, picking up rocks out here," supplied Luke.

Which was exactly how I'd have put it, if I'd thought of it.

"Instead of fossil ferns," suggested Luke, "how about lumps of coal? Like bad little boys and girls get in their stockings?"

"Lumps of coal would work," I allowed.

"We'll have to wait until dark," said Luke.

"I'll finish my homework in the meantime," I replied.

And so we started stealing coal from the Victory Fuels Corporation by sneaking around their shut-down mine at night and picking up all the stray chunks that had fallen between railroad ties and through cracks in the wall of the coal chute and places like that. Turned out, coal chunks were perfect for weighing down the skirts of a residential tent. Also, you could burn them to stay warm, if you did it at night so nobody from the company saw the smoke.

Preston started to cough again. So did a lot of people, actually. Being hungry, cold, tired, shot, and sad all at once will do that to you.

Dad got cracking building a wheelchair for Mom out of an old dining seat and the wheels off the bicycle Luke and I shared. He didn't ask to use the wheels, but Luke and I could both walk, unlike Mom, so we didn't complain.

Mom had never liked having help doing anything, and now, when I had to roll her to the table for breakfast, or reach high on a shelf to find the salt, her neck went stiff and her eyes focused on something far away.

Dad managed to locate a tire gauge, and he constantly

busied himself with the challenge of getting her inner tubes inflated to the proper level, like maybe, somehow, hitting on just the right air pressure would fix everything.

The shadow that fed on Preston's cough grew like a storm cloud over us. "I'm not complaining," he said one night before bed. And that was true. Preston had a nonstop mouth, but he never used it for complaining. "I'm just hungry."

The next day, coming back from Honey Brook with an armload of clean undershorts, some with Aristotle or Luke emblazoned on them in the indelible ink of Aristotle's black pen, I thought I saw a jackrabbit the size of an Irish setter lope through our camp. Looking back, I think hunger and desperation might have clouded my vision. Maybe he was only as big as a beagle. Either way, what he had written across his rear end in flashing Looney Tunes letters was DINNER!

"Luke!" I shouted. "Get out here!"

I heard his big Greek football feet clomp out of his tent. By then the bunny had looped into the desert and was heading toward the mountain south of town. Luke and I chased him, and as we skidded to a stop at the foot of Mount Hosta, we could see him perched on an outcrop shaped like the nose of a Roman emperor, watching us. I dug up a good clonker from a small rockslide that had tumbled down the slope, a stone about the size of a golf ball, and heavy, and jagged, and I let it fly. My throw was uphill, the jackrabbit was half a football field away, the sun shone in my eyes and the wind blew in my face, but one thing I *had* learned back in Low Ridge, Mississippi, was how to bean my own meals.

"Crackerjack!" applauded Luke, giving a whistle.

"Just—bringing home dinner," I mumbled.

"How'd you do it?" asked Luke.

"Well," I answered, keeping an eye on the slope above us in case a coyote happened to get wind of my handiwork and try to steal it, "the trick is—you just gotta hold your mouth right."

Luke picked up a rock. "How?" he asked.

I showed him.

"Stick your bottom teeth out from under your top ones," I advised, "and squinch your right eye more."

"But I'm left-handed," pointed out Luke.

"Then squinch your left eye," I amended.

He gave it a whirl.

At first, I couldn't even see what he was throwing at, but as his rock flew, I realized it was closing on a big fat pigeon winging overhead, and it bopped that bird right on the head. Down came the pigeon with a juicy plop somewhere near my rabbit on the ridge above us. I'd never seen anybody knock a bird out of the sky before.

"Okay, well, yeah," I said, "pretty good."

"Thanks," said Luke modestly.

"I mean, for your first try and everything," I added. "Let's go get 'em before the coyotes do."

The rabbit was giant. He didn't outweigh an Irish setter or collie, but he'd definitely have been able to whip certain beagles.

The pigeon was just right for a pie.

"Awwww," cooed Luke as I picked up my rabbit, his furry head lolling, his pink tongue sticking out. "He's cute."

"Um," I replied.

"We should name that bunny."

"But——" I said.

"Look at his big brown eyes!" Luke persisted. "I think we should call him——"

"Come on!" I protested. "Name him what?"

"Stew!" declared Luke. "Throw some carrots in there, maybe chop up an onion——"

"Stew. Good one," I had to admit.

"Sorry, Stew——" Luke told the rabbit.

"——better you than us," I said.

"Now what about the pigeon?" asked Luke, cradling him in two hands.

"Reginald," I said.

"Perfect," declared Luke.

I hefted the dead bunny, or as I liked to think of him,

dinner, and Luke turned around to clamber back down the outcrop, which looked very different from where we now stood.

"Which way do we go?" I asked.

"Down?" he suggested.

"Sure," I replied. "But *which* down?" Because it wasn't as simple as you'd have thought. Mount Hosta was complicated—splitting into ridges, spines, gorges, ravines, rockfalls, cliffs, and gullies as far as the eye could see. In the three minutes we hadn't been paying attention, we'd gotten ourselves completely lost.

"Maybe we could ask over there," suggested Luke, pointing at a perfect little house in a mountain meadow just visible over the next ridge like something from a fairy tale: peaked roof, red shutters, yellow window boxes, and green trim.

"If a weird old lady comes to the door and asks us in," whispered Luke as we knocked, "don't get between her and the oven."

A weird not-so-old lady came to the door. "Would you like to come in?" she asked. The mothball fumes billowing around her probably stunned migrating butterflies as far away as Mexico. "Leave your pets on the front porch if you don't mind."

Luke and I glanced at each other, but since there wasn't another mysterious mountain cottage handy, we dropped

Reginald and Stew in the grass and stepped inside that one. In the light, I got a good look at the woman who lived there. Behind eyeglasses as thick as the windshield of a spaceship, she had the same green eyes as the doctor who had saved all my friends. I was sure she must be Doc O'Malley's sister.

"I'm Josh Garrett, and this is my friend Luke Agrippa, ma'am," I said.

"Don't ma'am me, sir. I am *Miss* O'Malley," she snapped, scorching me with those peepers of hers, but not too much. "You may call me *Aunt* Bridey."

"But you're not our—" Luke started to point out.

"You may *call* me Aunt Bridey!" repeated Aunt Bridey in a tone that brooked no argument.

Luke scratched his head as if he was trying to put all this together, but I saw how it fit. She wasn't married. She'd never been married. Maybe she'd wanted to marry somebody once, and maybe one day she still would because she wasn't all that old. But for now she lived up here in her mountain meadow with her green eyes and probably some binoculars to spy on birds with and carried a fruitcake down the mountain to her brother and her nieces and nephews every holiday season so they wouldn't forget she existed, and the rest of the time she stayed up here wearing her essence of mothballs sweater and stayed out of everybody's affairs.

I shot Luke a look expressing all this.

"Right," he said. "Pardon the intrusion," he added. "If you could just direct us back to Victory, we'll be on our way."

"There," she said, pointing over the edge of a nearby cliff.

"I, ah, thanks," said Luke, eyeing it dubiously.

"Oh, don't be such a *sissy!*" chided Aunt Bridey. "The drop-off isn't as bad as it looks. And there's a trail. Leads past the beehive. Along the brook. Antelopes use it all the time."

"Thank you," I said.

On our way out, something on her hall table caught my eye: a photograph. A gauzy, faded photograph of a soldier not much older than I was, dressed in the ragged, dirty, gray uniform of the Confederate States Army. And beside the soldier stood, unmistakably, Aunt Bridey, when she was maybe fifteen years old.

SMACK! went the picture, facedown on the table, shattering the glass. Aunt Bridey glared at me, picking a shard out of her finger. "It's rude to stare at other people's personal effects," she snapped. "Now, if you don't mind, out!"

Luke and I obediently trooped through the door.

"Wait," she said, following. "I've got something for you."

I could tell Luke was expecting her to fork over a

handful of magic beans, or fetch a spinning wheel and weave for us an enchanted cloak, but instead she led us through an orchard of tiny, gnarled trees, arrayed like a hundred little old ladies on parade in her backyard. "Apricot orchard," said Aunt Bridey.

"Did you plant it?" asked Luke.

"No," she snapped. "Elves did it while I slept."

"I was just—" protested Luke.

"I know what you were just," shot back Aunt Bridey. "Now. Look here."

She led us to the face of a cliff looming over the northern border of her garden. Into the base of the cliff was bolted a wooden door. Aunt Bridey retrieved the key from atop the lintel. Behind the door, hidden in the cool shadows, were thousands of jars of apricot jelly.

"It's just me up here," she said, "and I have an overly large orchard. So I make a lot of preserves. About two hundred times more than I could spread on my toast over the next fifty years."

"But why—how do you—are you saying this is for us—are you on our side?" asked Luke.

"Despite these glasses, I'm not blind," she told us, glaring furiously past the edge of the cliff. "And I'm not deaf. I know what goes on. Don't touch the Honey Brook Nectar!" she added suddenly, as I reached toward a row of glass bottles on a high shelf. "And don't you dare tell the government about it!"

I knew from my days in Mississippi that this meant Honey Brook Nectar was actually moonshine.

"My bees make the honey from apricot blossoms and I make the nectar from the honey and it's off-limits!" emphasized Aunt Bridey.

Apricot blossom honey moonshine. "We won't tell the government, Aunt Bridey," I promised.

"And if you know what's good for you, you won't let anybody from the Victory Corporation find out I'm giving you jam," she added.

"We'll be careful, Aunt Bridey," Luke assured her.

"Good-bye!" she said, stalking back to her little house. "Take a bushel of those brussels sprouts from beside my porch when you go! And don't forget your dead animals."

Aunt Bridey's apricot jelly and the brussels sprouts helped. And Reginald and Stew made for one very nice dinner. But after that, without bread, or biscuits, or crackers, we just had to eat the jam with a spoon, and surprisingly, jam out of a spoon didn't make for a very satisfying meal. And brussels sprouts, well, when you get right down to it, they're nothing but brussels sprouts.

And the cold air blowing off the mountain got colder.

I gave Preston my blanket and managed to convince him I thought it was *fun* sleeping in my coat, boots, hat, and gloves, but still he got sick and then he got sicker.

Doc O'Malley, who didn't seem to notice the difference between the brick homes of Victory and the tents of Canvasburg when the people inside them were sick, listened to Preston's chest while he lay on his cot and said, "Double pneumonia. One, you need to keep him warm. And two, you need to feed him something besides apricot jam."

Luke, who had been hovering in the corner of our tent hanging on Doc O'Malley's every word, disappeared before he got to "two."

CHAPTER SEVEN

Margaret
2014

WE DON'T CALL IT A GIFT. I did once, entirely by accident. The word just slipped out the way words sometimes do when you're trying to read a book, eat a peppermint pattie, and have a conversation with your dad all at the same time. Big mistake. My dad whirled around, cobra fast, and corrected me so sharply that I swallowed the stupid pattie whole. Luckily it was fun-sized, even though there was nothing fun about it that day.

No, what most of us call it—when we talk about it, which isn't often—is "the quirk," sometimes "the O'Malley quirk" although that's not quite right because it's been paddling around in our gene pool for so long that there are plenty of people with other last names in our family who have it. Plus, rumor has it ("rumor" being mainly my uncle Joe) that other people totally unrelated to us have the quirk, too, or had it. Picasso, for one. Harriet Tubman, for another. But no one really knows that for sure. It could just be Uncle Joe, trying to lump us in with the important folks.

Lots of families have genetic quirks. Double-jointed thumbs. Perfect pitch. Synesthesia, where sounds and smells—and letters—or in the exceptionally cool case of Duke Ellington, musical notes, blossom into colors before your eyes. Heterochromia, where your eyes are two different colors; a girl named Iris (that was her name, no lie) on my field hockey team had this, and everyone was crazy jealous, including yours truly. Extra ribs. A photographic memory, which some scientists say doesn't even exist but which seems to run in families all the same.

My family has time travel.

As for how it works, well, all I can tell you is what my dad told me. It's not magic, exactly, although parts of it seem pretty magical. So do a lot of natural occurrences, though, when you think about it: the Northern Lights, those people who can reel off prime numbers up to six digits the way you and I would recite the multiplication table, the speed of light, black holes, monarch migration, and practically every single thing bees ever do.

My dad gave me the scoop the day after my tenth birthday. It wasn't some big, ceremonious presentation, no "now my child, I will pass down the wisdom of the ages" type of thing, and he was really careful not to scare me. But he was serious for sure, especially when he swore me to secrecy. "Not even Charlie," he told me, which is how I knew he meant business.

We were sitting on our front porch eating leftover cake. Every now and then, while he was talking, my dad would sketch pictures in the air with his fork or draw a little diagram on his napkin. Since my dad's not such a great drawer, this wasn't so helpful, but that was okay because he is an excellent explainer.

Here's what he said:

"Time isn't just one long tunnel all of us humans travel down, keeping each other company inside while we're alive, and that we leave behind for the rest to keep on exploring when we die."

Honestly, I hadn't thought much about the nature of time before, but if I had, I would've described it more or less the way he just had, so I said, "It's not?"

"Nope. Time is a garden hose stuffed in a suitcase."

I laughed.

"No kidding," said my dad. "An infinitely long garden hose stuffed into a very big suitcase, a suitcase larger than just about everything you can think of, including our universe."

"That's big."

"Yep. And the hose is stuffed in such a way that every bit

of it is touching every other bit of it, if you can imagine that."

I tried. "I can't."

"That's okay, I can't either. But the point is that every bit of time is actually curled up cozily beside us, all day every day, even if it is hopelessly, eternally just out of reach. Out of reach *unless*—and here's where things get tricky, so please pay attention—you figured out a way to poke a pinhole in the walls of the hose, those walls being otherwise known as the limits of reality as we know them, and you slipped through the pinhole from one loop to the next in an instant."

"Yeah, but nobody could do that," I scoffed.

It's possible that I rolled my eyes at this point, because my dad said, "Once you've stopped rolling your eyes, ladybug, do me a favor."

"What?"

"Picture your average pair of workout pants."

I laughed, again.

"Or shirt. Actually, any item of breathable, high-performance athletic apparel will do. When you look at your item, it appears to be all one piece, right? But actually, it's *full of holes*, exactly like . . . can you guess?"

I shook my head.

"*The fabric of the universe!* Everything you see around you is at least as much not-there as it is there. The spaces between the particles inside the atoms that make up your own body? Huge, like the distances between the stars in the Milky Way. The pinholes in the garden hose? No need to poke them yourself; they're already there, at least until they close up. The basic material of reality is all loosely connected and shifting, the tiny bits shimmering and scattering into holes that flash open and shut, blinking all around us."

I tried to picture this, and, weirdly, I could. So I nodded.

My dad continued. "The problem is that almost nobody can see the blinking holes because most people's perception is as holey as everything else. You know those flip books? The ones with a picture on every page, pictures that vary just a little, so that when the pages are turned quickly, the pictures turn into a kind of animated cartoon?"

"I made one in art class," I said. "Remember? The guy diving off the edge of the soup bowl and swimming around with the dumplings."

"I do remember. The animation with those books, even one as excellent as yours was, tends to be a little herky-jerky, but if you added more pages and flipped faster, it would smooth out, look continuous, tell a story. Same goes for perception. Take Mr. Yang, for instance."

My dad nodded in the direction of our neighbor, who was running down our street, like he did every weekend morning, listening to his iPod and dancing to the music just ever so slightly. I smiled.

"Take him where?" I said.

"Ha ha. Your eyes are seeing him at just ten frames per second, which is pretty herky-jerky, but your brain is guessing what's in those blank spaces and is kindly filling them in for you, adding pages to the flip book, so that Mr. Yang's running looks seamless, smooth as silk."

"Well, except for the dancing," I said.

"In situations like these, your brain usually guesses correctly, but there's always the chance that in one of the gaps, Mr. Yang doesn't keep running, but instead jumps—at lightning speed—twenty feet in the air, grabs a Frisbee out of the sky with his teeth, and flings it into the distance. And you miss it because your eyes don't see it and your brain guesses that he won't grab a Frisbee, that he'll just plain run, with a few dance moves thrown in. Get it?"

"I think so."

"Similarly, your brain guesses that in one of the gaps between frames in whatever you happen to be seeing, a pinhole in the form of a portal into the past *doesn't* blink open and shut. So you miss it, the portal, as though it were never there because, for you, it never was. Unless you're an O'Malley."

At this, I jerked my head around to look at my dad. He nodded.

"Or a Picasso or a Tubman, if Uncle Joe is to be believed, which maybe he isn't. If you've got the O'Malley quirk, your big, odd, glass-green eyes, at least while you're young, before your eyesight starts to fade, can see things other people's eyes don't."

"Like what?"

"Like way more pages of the flip book than other people can see. Like the Frisbee between the teeth and the blinking holes in time."

"Whoa."

"Whoa is right. But even we don't see this stuff all the time, because how would that be? Can you imagine it?"

I imagined it. Images coming at me from every direction all the time, bombarding my brain. I shivered at the thought. My dad grabbed a piece of my hair and gently tugged it, which was one of his versions of a hug.

"People would shut down, short out, freak, right? The O'Malleys, too. The good news is that, under ordinary circumstances, our brains block out all but what we need to know in order to function in an ordinary way. On a daily basis, we perceive more or less what everyone else does. But unlike everyone else, we can deliberately put ourselves in *extra*ordinary circumstances, in exactly the right position and mood and frame of mind to, well, *travel*."

"Travel," I said, wonderingly, turning over the word in my mind. "Time travel?"

My dad nodded. "We can see the holes in time, choose the one we want, and slip through, quick as a mongoose, into the past. Possibly also into the future, although no one seems to know about that, which probably means either that we can't do it, we just don't see those portals, or that if any O'Malley ever has done it, she or he hasn't, uh, well . . ."

"Lived to tell the tale," I finished, grimly.

"Anyway, traveling is something we have to choose to do. Or choose not to do."

And this is where the forswearing came in, the words generations of O'Malleys promised to live by, even if we knew they weren't precisely true:

> *There is one Now: the spot where I stand,*
> *And one way the road goes: onward, onward.*

I forswore for the first time that day, and my dad would have me repeat it from time to time over the years, just for good measure. Everyone takes the vow. Nobody breaks the vow.

But, after my conversation with Grandpa Joshua about changing the past, saving Aristotle and therefore Luke and therefore (oh please, please) my dad, as I rode home from Charlie's house, blindly, wildly zigzagging down the road like a bat in sunlight, I began to consider the possibility— and it was a terrifying one—that that "Nobody" might not include me.

CHAPTER EIGHT

Josh
1938

BY THE TIME DOC O'MALLEY finally took Preston to the infirmary and told the nurse at the desk, "Just admit him, he's a little boy, for Pete's sake, I'll pay the bill!" food was running low for all of us. I went to ask Luke to hike up the mountain with me for more jam and possibly squash, but he was nowhere to be found.

So I went by myself. It wasn't exactly a Sunday school picnic. The Model T tank was long gone, but there was no shortage of alleged detectives lurking around to make sure none of us broke any of the new rules in effect after what Biggs and the company called the "Canvasburg Uprising," which was *their* name for the machine-gun attack, rules like no sneaking out of Canvasburg.

Unbeknownst to the detectives, who weren't the smartest bunch, Aristotle and sometimes the Kowalski brothers or my dad were still climbing over the mountains at night to mail our letters, and once in a while they brought back boxes packed by kind folks from towns as far away as Arden, Delaware, and Oneida, New York, full of sweaters, canned beans, and notes of encouragement. A church in Philadelphia even mailed us three live chickens. It was nice to realize people across the United States understood our plight.

The chickens managed to escape from their crate in the middle of camp, and after that they roamed free, laying eggs under random tumbleweeds.

I bet Biggs would've made chickens against the rules if he could've. It drove him crazy, the way we crept around and held on and managed to keep ourselves alive.

So I waited until the detective watching us that morning went off to buy cigarettes, and I ducked into the trees beside Honey Brook and sneaked behind them into Honey Canyon and waded up the stream until I was hidden from Victory, and then I hiked to Aunt Bridey's.

The cold had let up that morning, and with the sun beating down on me, I ended up panting by the time I got there. I found Aunt Bridey's door ajar, so I walked in. I could hear her clattering around in the kitchen, but before I got around to announcing I was there, I noticed the picture she'd slammed onto its face the day I'd met her. She'd set it upright again, so I took the opportunity to look it over in detail. While I did, she lurched in, carrying a drink the color of honey, a glazed look in her eye. "I've got twenty-five pounds of potatoes you can have, in a basket under the porch," she said. She stopped short when she found me staring at the photo.

"I was young once, just like you," Aunt Bridey said.

This revelation stretched my imagination farther than just about any concept that'd come up since I'd left Low Ridge, Mississippi, but I managed to keep my trap shut.

"Don't look so shocked!" she snapped. "I don't mean I was *just* like you. Nobody I knew was in danger, nor was I. Truth is, I'd have envied you. You're brave and you have challenges to meet—"

"I wish I didn't," I murmured.

"I know," said Aunt Bridey as kindly as I ever heard her say anything. "I was a silly girl. I craved excitement. I hankered for adventure. I felt sure I'd been born to bigger things than my life here."

"Here?" I asked, pointing at the floor under my feet like some kind of idiot who, from time to time, loses track of where he happens to be standing.

"This house," Aunt Bridey continued. "I was raised in it, back when my little vegetable patch was a whole farm. Before the Victory Corporation forced my father's spread out from under him because there was coal buried in it. I grew up during the quiet years, which I felt were far too quiet."

She glanced at the photo of herself and the soldier. No slamming it on its face today.

"So you went looking for an interesting friend," I supplied. "You went to a Halloween party with that guy who wore a Confederate costume?"

"I went looking for an interesting *time*," she corrected, "inhabited by Lieutenant Walker, of the Confederate States Army, whose uniform was anything *but* a costume."

I took a long look at Lieutenant Walker. He had that look in his eyes, the stare, the expression only real soldiers in real pictures from the Civil War ever had, because they had to stand in rows and shoot their own neighbors and sometimes their own brothers.

"Deserter, visionary, hero. A young man with a dream," continued Aunt Bridey, "that I thought I was going to help bring to life."

"Wait—" I stammered, doing the math. By my calculations, Aunt Bridey couldn't have been more than forty years old. "How were you going to help him, if he was in the Civil War? I mean, you weren't born yet."

Bridey just stared at me with her fizzing eyes like she was deciding something about me. Then she gazed back at the picture. "I left myself this daguerreotype as a souvenir," she said. "I couldn't bring it through time with me, because that's not allowed, so I hid it in a corner of that cave out back, and it waited for me through the years."

"Where'd you stash it—next to the time machine?" I joked. Aunt Bridey was making me nervous. "Does H. G. Wells live across the creek?"

"Time machine," she scoffed. "H. G. Wells was an idiot. He didn't know the first thing about time travel."

"Hold on." I realized I halfway believed her. The photo was so strange—and of course, so was Aunt Bridey. "What are you telling me?"

"I traveled through time," she said evenly. "And made a friend who was as brave as anyone in history. But after what you and Luke did in the face of that gunfire, you might be his equal."

"Aunt Bridey?" I pleaded, confused and a little scared. "Why are you telling me this?"

"Because I want you to realize," she replied, "that I understand time backward, forward, and inside out. And I understand friendship, too."

"So—" I began.

"So I know beyond the shadow of a doubt," she said, fixing my eyes with hers, "that friendship will stand the test of time."

"I see," I said slowly.

"I doubt it," she said. "Not now. But you will."

"Thank you, Aunt Bridey," I gulped. "I think."

"You're welcome," she replied, "I think. Now: Never tell a soul about this. If you do, I'll just say you're crazy."

"You would know." I grinned. But I stopped grinning as my mind took off going ninety to nothing, considering all the angles, because if she could really time travel, then maybe she could slip back to the night before the gun opened up on my friends, and maybe she could pilfer the ammunition, or maybe she could sabotage the gun, or maybe, or maybe . . .

"Now don't go getting any ideas," Aunt Bridey warned, "because I can't travel anymore. And even if I could, I wouldn't."

"Why not?"

"There's something my relatives have to say about that—since the ability runs in our blood, we made a family rule:

> *There is one Now: the spot where I stand,*
> *And one way the road goes: onward, onward . . .*

". . . you get the idea . . ." She trailed off.

"You're drunk, aren't you?" I said.

"Possibly," she said. She poured out her nectar in a nearby flowerpot. "But I'm not crazy. Now take your potatoes and go. At least"—she added as I turned to leave— "you're in no danger from that awful Tin Lizzie anymore."

"That what?" I asked.

"That tank Biggs's thugs shot at you with. One of my

goats got out yesterday. Had to track him to Humboldt Draw to catch him. Those idiots stashed their Model T behind a boulder there. It won't be going anywhere anytime soon. Oscar ate all four tires."

"Oscar?" I asked.

"My goat," replied Aunt Bridey.

"Which way is Humboldt Draw?" I asked as I headed out the door.

She told me.

"I'll be back later for the potatoes!" I hollered over my shoulder.

When I got back to Canvasburg, I realized where Luke had been that morning—jail. As soon as he'd heard the doc say we needed to keep Preston warm, he'd run off to steal more coal, but by then, we'd picked up everything in sight. So by the light of dawn, Luke fired up the elevator all by himself and went clattering down to the mine to do his collecting. Maybe he wasn't thinking straight because he was flustered about Preston. Maybe he wanted to provoke the company. Whatever he hoped to accomplish, when he came back up, the sheriff and Elijah Biggs were waiting for him.

But before Luke spent too long in the clink, Aristotle got the sheriff to release him, since he was just a kid. I met them coming back from the sheriff's office. Luke was shouting, "But Preston was gonna die! Doc O'Malley said!"

"Preston's in the infirmary," Aristotle said.

"He's safe," I threw in. Startled, they noticed me for the first time. "He can have food and medicine. Doc O'Malley made them admit him."

"Son, you act too hasty," Aristotle admonished Luke.

"I just wanted to keep him warm," protested Luke.

"I know. It was a brave thing. You try. But why you start that elevator, where everybody can hear? Why you go looking for a fight?" asked Aristotle.

Luke stiffened. "The fight came looking for *me*," he retorted. "It came looking for all of us. You just won't let us fight it!"

We walked past the company store. A couple of customers strolled out. People from Victory. Lawyers, accountants, folks like that. Folks who still had money for food. The baker must've just pulled his bread out of the oven. The aroma was enough to drive a starving kid nuts.

"You know what this is, Dad?" Luke demanded, digging a brass key out of his pocket.

"I don't wanna know," said Aristotle.

"It's the key to the sheriff's gun cabinet. He just leaves it in his top drawer, and while you were promising him you'd keep me out of trouble, I stole it. And guess what?"

"I can't," said Aristotle tiredly as we neared Canvasburg.

"I'm gonna go into camp, and tell Mr. Martinelli and everybody else, and we're gonna steal those guns, and rob the company store tonight, and we're gonna eat, and after that, we're gonna—"

Aristotle snatched the key from Luke and threw it what looked like half a mile, over the tents, out into the desert. Which was as close as I'd ever seen him to losing his temper.

"You never listen to me!" exploded Luke. "You never pay attention to me! You never take me when you go do things at night, and you never let me help!"

"You brave!" cried Aristotle. "You good! I love you! And I'm doing this for you, my Luke!"

"I found the tank!" I shouted. I wanted to put a stop to this argument. I wanted to help Aristotle. I wanted to help Luke. So I said, "It'll get reporters here, won't it? It's what we need to show the world what happened? It's evidence of what happened, right? A goat ate the tires, but the rest is still there."

"Josh!" said Aristotle. "My boy! Where is it?"

We were almost back to Canvasburg. But I glanced around, just in case a stray detective happened to be nearby detecting. The coast was clear. I told Aristotle: Humboldt Draw.

"I'm going over the mountains tonight to send a telegram," declared Aristotle. "To tell Walter Mendenhall.

He'll ride the train from Denver. He'll bring Milton Katz, the great photographer. It's gonna happen."

"Aw, that's just peachy!" burst out Luke in disgust. "I get thrown in jail, and swipe the key to all the guns, and Josh comes up with some story about a goat, and he's the one you listen to?"

"I told you: no guns!" admonished Aristotle. "Now good-bye, son. I gotta go."

"Let me come with you, Dad!" Luke begged. "This time, just once, let me?"

"You better not, Luke," said Aristotle. "You stay here. They catch me doing this, they don't put me in the jail, they put me *under* the jail."

"Dad," pleaded Luke. "I want to help."

"Then you do what I tell you," replied Aristotle, like dads say to their kids every day all over the world.

Aristotle sneaked away from camp as soon as the sun set. We heard gunshots on the mountain, but all we could do was hope it was Mr. Martinelli hunting or the detectives plugging tin cans with their pistols by moonlight.

Luke sat alone in his tent.

Since Aristotle was on his mission to telegraph the reporters, my dad went to mail the day's letters and to bring back whatever replies had come to the Mercury post office.

He came home with a crumpled box addressed to Preston. It appeared to be from Germantown, Pennsylvania.

"Who could've sent it?" speculated my mom. "I wonder if it's dangerous."

"Let's see," said Preston, chipper again after a warm night of infirmary blankets and a hot breakfast, ripping it open to find a dented old trumpet wrapped in a sweater.

By afternoon, Aristotle was still not back. To boost Luke's spirits, Preston had learned to play "When the Saints Go Marching In," clutching the trumpet in the ruins of his right hand, his left fingers smacking the valves open and shut faster than the human eye could follow. A message stuck to the horn had read, "For Aristotle's young friend." I guess Aristotle must've written somebody in Germantown to ask if they could spare an instrument playable by a kid with only seven fingers, and they'd sent this old trumpet.

Elijah Biggs materialized at the door of the tent. This was a first; he'd never been seen in Canvasburg before. Most of the time, he did his best to pretend it didn't exist. "A trumpet," he observed. "Now where, I wonder, did a trumpet come from?"

"Germantown, Pennsylvania," shot back Luke.

"Really," sniffed Biggs, glancing around as if he smelled something foul. "Somehow, you've persuaded the fine people of Germantown, Pennsylvania, to feel sorry for you. I wonder how?"

Preston stopped playing.

"I notice your father is nowhere to be found," observed Biggs.

"That's because right now he's—"

And I'm pretty sure that Luke was within half a second of telling Biggs exactly where his father was and what he was up to—

So I said, "Fishing! Aristotle went fishing!"

A look of chagrin crossed Luke's face as he realized he'd been about to reveal our plans to Biggs. Biggs looked amused.

"Well, then," said Biggs smoothly to me, "I'll just have to admire his catch when he gets back. Although what kind of a yellowbelly goes off fishing while his friends are in such trouble—"

Luke moved so fast, I never saw how his hands got around Biggs's throat. It wasn't easy to pry him loose, since he weighed about twice as much as I did and was as strong as most coal miners. Luckily, the sheriff and Biggs's two flunkys were there to restrain him.

"I'm not going to press charges." Biggs chuckled, straightening his pastel tie. "If you ask me, the boy's got the right idea, fighting his own fights, even if he's on the wrong side."

Preston launched into "Ain't Misbehavin'," which was a joke aimed at Elijah Biggs, since if you asked Preston, he was *always* misbehaving. Biggs must've gotten the joke, because he turned around and stalked back to his brick office in disgust.

When he was safely gone, Biggs's men let Luke go.

To take Luke's mind off his dad, and Biggs, and everything else, I said, "Let's go to Bridey's. She's got a bushel of potatoes we need to bring down."

But instead of lugging the bushel basket back home right away, Luke and I gazed down the mountain, at Canvasburg, where all our friends and family were sad, and hungry, and shot, and in wheelchairs, and sick, and angry.

And I looked the other way, and said, "What do you think is up there?"

"Don't know," replied Luke. "Never been."

"We'll get back quick," I said, and with that, Luke and I scampered up the slope.

There was a trail between the desert rocks, left by deer or antelope, or maybe the forefathers of the Navajo who lived around there, and sometimes it got so steep we had to crawl. Things began to change as we got higher—the air thinned out and freshened on our faces and billowed in our shirts, and the heat from all the climbing evaporated right out of us and wafted up to the clouds.

Up. Up is great. Nobody had ever told me about Up. Once you start Up, there's just no stopping. Sure, my lungs seemed to be turning to sawdust. Sure, it felt like somebody had strung barbed wire through my hamstrings and started tightening it with a crowbar. But—

"Feel okay?" shouted Luke over his shoulder, bounding up the incline like a mountain goat.

"Oh yeah," I wheezed.

"Need to stop?" asked Luke.

"Oh no," I gasped.

"'Cause my legs are kind of tired," Luke allowed.

Mine weren't just tired. They felt like they might have to be amputated. Luckily, the waves of dizziness washing over me took my mind off the pain. "Come on," I shouted, sprinting past him toward the base of a granite cliff. "Look! The top is right here!"

Of course the top wasn't right there. When we got over the lip of the cliff, the mountain just kept right on stretching away from us, onward and upward.

"What do you know about that?" mused Luke.

"What do you know is right," I agreed, and kept on hiking. I was sure we'd get to the summit soon, because I'd never before seen anything I couldn't walk across in ten minutes. They didn't call Low Ridge, Mississippi, "Low Ridge" for nothing. It was three feet high. You could basically step right over it. This mountain went on for miles.

The desert stones became a meadow. The meadow changed to brush. The brush gave way to trees. The trees grew thicker. Streams began to flow all around us. Pine needles carpeted the ground.

"We're in a forest," I observed, staring at the pines, which were now almost as tall as the ones back in Mississippi. "In the desert." Pines turned to oaks, and the oaks began to shed their leaves: yellow, red, and orange.

"If somebody shoots at you," asked Luke philosophically, "shouldn't you shoot back?"

"I don't know," I answered. Maybe, not long before, I'd have said yes without a doubt. But after listening to Aristotle, I wasn't so sure. "I don't think—maybe not."

"But—if somebody kills somebody," Luke went on, eyeing me sideways, "shouldn't they have to pay?"

"Yes," I said, because on this point I was clear.

"Shouldn't *we* make *them* pay?" continued Luke, stopping to look at me. His eyes were imploring. "Because nobody else is going to."

"We?" I repeated. "Us?" Luke turned away, and we climbed higher. The air bit. Our lungs burned. The tree branches above us thinned, and through them I spotted a blue so dark, I imagined I could see space behind it.

"We're *right*!" said Luke, ignoring my questions as he

thought about his own. "They're *wrong!*" Suddenly, we walked right out of the forest onto—bare rock—and then snow—and just like that, it was winter on Mount Hosta.

"Look," I said. "The peak." No more surprises. No more mountain hiding behind the mountain. This was it. Snow surrounded the stony summit. We could see sky on the left and the right and above us.

"We're right," persisted Luke, "so we're supposed to *win!*"

"True," I replied.

"But," Luke went on, "how can we win if we don't fight? My dad says no. He always says no." Luke's voice trailed off as we realized that, from the top of the mountain, we could see the earth in *every* direction. We stood on an island in the sky in silence.

"It's all ours!" I finally said. "Our mountain. Our desert. Our forests and our rivers. The whole world."

"And we're the kings of it all," crowed Luke.

"And we can change it," I continued.

"You and me," said Luke excitedly. "We really could, Josh. I know it!" Then he looked at me curiously. "But how?"

"Your dad, Luke," I said. "He knows a lot—maybe he's trying to show us. I think if we listen to him, he could teach us how."

And that is where I lost Luke Agrippa.

"He's not as smart as people think," muttered Luke, staring at something far away that I couldn't see. "I don't even understand what he's talking about sometimes. How are we supposed to take away the occasion of all wars? What does that mean?"

I fell silent, because I didn't know. Behind us, over a mountain range so far west it might have been in California, the sun disappeared, leaving only a fading glow above us. "The light is going!" I cried. "We gotta get home!"

"I guess we do," agreed Luke quietly, disappointed that I couldn't answer his questions.

I sort of figured going down would be faster than climbing up, and it was. I also figured going down would be easier, and there's where I was mistaken. Sadly. When you're pelting down the side of a mountain, those rocks come at you fast. I spent as much time sliding on my face as running, and Luke was bleeding from both knees and both elbows by the time we got back to the tree line. When we dropped out of the forest, the sun had completely set. We grabbed Bridey's potatoes and kept running. We had only stars to see by.

And before we got back to camp, Aristotle had already sneaked in with Walter Mendenhall and Milton Katz. Milton Katz, eluding the detectives, snapped a photo of the Model T, which people had a hard time believing was real when they saw it in the *Weekly World Worker*. But he also snapped a picture of Preston, standing in front of our tent, blowing taps on his trumpet at dusk. Of course in the photo you couldn't tell he was playing taps, but then again, you kind of could, and something about Preston standing straight as a soldier holding the dented horn with his ruined hand caught everybody's eye, because that picture ended up in the *New York Times*, and millions of people saw it.

CHAPTER NINE

Margaret
2014

I HALF EXPECTED CHARLIE TO show up at my door a few minutes after I left, asking about the little time-travel bombshell Grandpa Joshua had dropped, but *only* half expected or maybe less than that. Maybe a quarter expected. Charlie would have been as perplexed, curious, and worried as the next guy, but he knew me, knew how I liked being alone for a while after something big and scary happened to me, even back when the biggest, scariest things were a C on a math test or a missed goal in a field hockey game. But even Charlie can't be patient forever, so that night at midnight, when I heard the pathetically bad mourning dove call outside my window, I was ready for it.

When I got to The Octagon, Charlie was lying on his back, gazing at the sky. I plopped down a few feet away. The stars beamed, calm and faraway and normal, but I felt weirdly shy around them now, like they were a person I couldn't quite look in the eye. So I rolled sideways to look at Charlie and propped myself up on my elbow. My head felt heavy as a bowling ball, like it was too full of stuff, which of course it was.

"Hey," I said.

"Hey," he said, still staring skyward.

"Hey, remember how we watched the Perseid meteor shower last summer?"

"Yeah."

"Remember how I counted, like, five times as many falling stars as you did?"

"Nope. And they aren't stars, genius."

"It's a figure of speech, genius."

It was amazing, that night, the points of light sliding down the sky like raindrops down a car window. Even though we knew better, there was no way not to expect them to fall on us in flurries, to get snagged in the tree branches, to clatter onto The Octagon and lie glowing in the long grass of the field; that's how personal it all seemed, how close and just for us.

I let myself slip back to that night, not like a time traveler, just like a regular girl, remembering. Then I flopped back down on my back, shut my eyes, and started to talk. I gave him everything, the whole spiel, mixed metaphors and all. The garden hose, the flip book, the holes blinking like eyes, and it wasn't until I was finished that I realized what I'd just done, how big it was, how risky. I'd just given Charlie the unbelievable and asked him to believe it. I'd just told him I had the ability to travel through time.

I sneaked a peek at him. In the dark, I could just see his face as he looked down at the tops of his own knees, his eyebrows lowered in a way that meant he was thinking something through. I lay there, hearing my pulse in my ears, waiting to find out if my best friend thought I was a liar or a lunatic, to find out whether he was still my best friend at all. I'd never felt so lonely in my life.

Finally, Charlie said, "What if you just go back and stop the people who really burned down the lab? I mean, we know the date and more or less the time. Wouldn't that be simpler than jumping all the way back to 1938?"

For a few seconds, I was too relieved to speak. *Maybe I can do this*, I thought. *If Charlie and I are in it together, I just might be able to pull it off.* If I hadn't known it would have embarrassed him to death, I would've cried or hugged Charlie. Or both.

Instead, I swallowed hard and said, "You can't travel in your own lifetime. That's what my dad told me. Two yous can't be together in a single now."

"That's good," said Charlie with a snort. "One you is plenty."

I punched him in the shoulder.

He ignored me, scrambled to a sitting position, and went on, getting excited, "So the next question is: *when* should you jump to? Grandpa Joshua seemed to be saying that if we stopped the murder in the hunting lodge, that would do the trick. But what if we stopped the whole Canvasburg massacre? What if we stole the guards' guns or stopped the kid from throwing the rock, if he really did throw one? We could save a lot of lives that way, right? *Including* Aristotle's. I mean, I guess that would save Aristotle, right?"

I liked the way he said "we," but I realized it was time to tell Charlie the next bit of information about time travel, the big, the vague, the spooky, the hard-to-get-your-mind-around-just-take-it-on-faith part (as if all the rest had been so easy to get your mind around). The part about the forces of history.

"I know, Charlie," I said, and at the sound of his name, he snapped his head up to look at me. Like most people who talked to each other all the time and didn't live on a movie screen, we only used each other's names in conversation when something big was coming up.

"It would be great to think big, to try to save everyone we can, to change all the bad stuff," I went on, gearing up to tell Charlie the spooky part but also wanting to put it off as long as possible, "but here's the thing, and I know this sounds kind of strange, but everyone says it, my dad, Uncle Joe, all of them, it's the reason for the forswearing, or, like one of the reasons, the main one probably, I mean there's also something in there about staying humble, not getting too full of ourselves and treating the quirk like a gift so that we start to think we're a bunch of superheroes or whatever—"

I stopped for breath.

"Just say it already," said Charlie, "whatever it is."

I sat up.

"History resists," I told him.

"Oh yeah, you said that yesterday. What's it mean?"

"History doesn't want to be messed with. It pushes back when you try."

"Pushes how?"

I sighed.

"Well, that's where people get a little hazy on the details. I mean, my family's been forswearing for a really long time, so maybe no one knows for sure, but what everyone's pretty clear on is that *history resists*."

"So," Charlie ventured, quietly, "maybe it's not going to work, you changing history to save your dad?"

It had to work. It had to, it had to, it had to.

"I don't know," I said.

We sat there, deflated. I don't know what was going on inside Charlie's head, but what I was doing was searching for a reason, any reason but preferably a good one, to hope. Then it hit me.

"But here's the thing," I said. "If it were impossible, why would we be able to travel at all? If history were that strong, wouldn't it stop us?"

Charlie looked at me, nodding. "Maybe. And 'resists' isn't exactly the same thing as 'prevents,' is it?"

"No way!"

"Okay, so it's worth a try."

"Definitely! But maybe what we should do is think small, just try to change one thing. I mean, no one really knows what triggered the massacre, so let's focus on the murder in the hunting lodge. We know the time and place. We can guess what happened."

Charlie nodded again and said, "It's small and contained and doesn't involve that many people—unlike, say, the massacre itself. Maybe if we don't get too ambitious and just really limit the change you make, history won't . . ."

"Notice?" I supplied. "Interfere? Get too mad?"

Charlie laughed, and I joined in. The whole thing was so serious and so crazy at the same time.

"Something like that," said Charlie.

"It's true. I need to have as small an impact on the past as possible."

"So you should probably stay out of sight as much as you can, not talk to a lot of people, and be there for as short a time as possible. The bare minimum."

"Supposedly, you can't stay that long anyway."

"How long is 'that long'?"

"Um, I'm not sure."

"Oh. Well, what happens if you stay too long?"

"Also not sure. Something not good, I guess?"

"Oh."

And all the possible "not good" things that could happen were suddenly all around us, creeping, closing in, casting ugly shadows across us. You think thoughts like that, about the unknown "not good" for too long, they can suck you down like quicksand, but it's also really hard to stop.

"I wish I could go instead of you," Charlie said in a low, dead-serious voice.

"Thanks," I said lightly. "I'll be fine, though. I'm tough."

The light tone was meant to make things better, relieve the tension, drive the "not good" back to wherever it came from, but like most things that are sort of faked, it backfired.

"You're *tough*?" said Charlie, angrily. "Seriously? You know what? Just because we aren't talking about how dangerous this is doesn't mean it's not. It's *insanely* dangerous. You could go through the wrong blinking hole and get lost in some random time. You could get stuck in 1938. And even if the time travel works, you're headed straight for a very messed-up situation. Guns, armored cars, a guy getting stabbed, another guy getting bashed over the head."

"Charlie—"

"No!"

He jumped to his feet, started to pace The Octagon.

"Forget it. This is wrong. *Dead* wrong!"

"Calm down," I said.

He stopped pacing and looked hard at me.

"You can't do it."

My jaw tightened the way it always does when someone tells me this.

"You can't stop me."

Charlie made a disgusted sound and shook his head. At this point, if I had been Charlie, I might have brought up my mom. I might have pointed out that the last thing she needed was to have her husband sentenced to death and then have her daughter disappear off the face of the earth— or at least earth circa 2014. Not that he needed to because I had already tortured myself with this thought enough, but he could have done it anyway, twisted the knife, gone for the low blow. Most people would have.

But Charlie said, wearily, "Look, I know you need to go and do this. I just wish you didn't have to do it alone."

"But I won't be alone," I said.

Charlie looked at me, puzzled.

"I'll be with Grandpa Joshua," I said. "The first thing I'll do is find him. And he's a pretty great guy."

Charlie let this sink in, smiled a ghost of a smile, and sat down.

"Okay," he said. "When?"

"I need a day," I said. "Just to hang out with my mom. So I guess tomorrow night at midnight."

"Where?"

"It's supposed to be a place where you feel relaxed and at home. So, here."

"How? And wait, why do you even know how? If no one is supposed to do it, why would your dad even tell you?"

"Because even though it's something you usually have to do on purpose, it's possible to do it by accident. Which would be terrible."

"Oh wow. Yeah, it would. Okay, how?"

So I told him. I started this way: "The first thing you do is give yourself to the universe. . . ."

My day with my mom was one of those things so through-and-through fine, so every-second sweet, that you mostly need to keep it to yourself, but I want you to know that it started with her coming downstairs after her shower, looking pale as a lily but clear-eyed and fresh, like someone who's just gone out walking in the cleanest rain ever and steps through the door and is home.

Some moms might have said "sorry" for having been out of commission for so long, but she didn't. This made me happy, because what did she have to be sorry about? Loving my dad so much? Hating injustice so much? Being worn out and sad? She might as well have apologized for being a human being, and no one should ever apologize for that.

Instead she said, "Here's the deal: you're my girl, I'm your mom, and we are going to bake."

It was a cinnamon-scented day, the kind you slip into your pocket, carry with you when you leave, and never lose.

My dad told me to begin outside, in the middle of the night when the sky is black and the stars are out, in a place that feels yours, where you feel safe and at home. He told me how you relax every muscle, letting go of anything that might hold you back, keep you tied to the Now—memories, fear, whatever song is on a replay loop inside your head, your itchy mosquito bite, thoughts of revenge, hope, hate, love (although he said love is supposed to be hardest of all)—and giving yourself, every little bit, to the universe, dropping yourself, body, heart, soul, mind, into the Everything like you'd drop a coin into an open palm.

He told me about the stars, how you watch them and only them, as they wheel in their ancient, complicated patterns, marking the seasons, the years, until you feel their wheelings and their cold, blue beauty inside you. He told me how they teach you about time, even though you're not aware of learning or even what you've learned. You're like a piece of paper the stars write the workings of time on in a language you don't know (or don't know you know) how to read. And he told me about how the one thought you hold in your mind so hard and repeat to yourself so many times that you begin to breathe it in and out and your heart begins to beat it is a date, the day you want to travel to.

When I walked out my door at 11:30 that night to make my shaky, sweaty-palmed way to The Octagon, Charlie was sitting on my porch with a bag.

"I Googled girls' clothes in 1938 and found some stuff in Jane's closet that might work."

Jane was Charlie's sixteen-year-old sister who had so many clothes that her room was more like a clothes museum than like a bedroom, if there are such things as clothes museums. She shopped everywhere, from thrift stores to fancy boutiques; half the stuff hanging in her closet (and sitting in boxes and thrown around her room) still had tags on it.

"Oh, wow, I didn't even think about what I'd wear!" I said.

Charlie tapped his head and winked in a way that meant, *Luckily, your best friend is a genius who thinks of everything.* I rolled my eyes and grabbed the bag out of his hand. Inside was a green-flowered cotton dress with a Peter Pan collar that buttoned up the front and a pair of brown-and-white saddle shoes that were two sizes too big for me.

"I'll look like an oversized baby with gigantic feet," I protested.

"Yeah, you're right. It'll be a lot better for you to show up in a hoodie, purple jeans, and neon-yellow running shoes," said Charlie.

I stuck my tongue out at him, snatched the clothes, and turned to go inside to change.

"Wait," said Charlie. "You're going to late October, right?"

"October 26, 1938," I said dutifully.

We'd decided that I'd go the day before the meeting in the hunting lodge, which we hoped would give me time to find Grandpa Joshua, convince him I wasn't a psycho, just a perfectly ordinary girl time traveling from 2014 to save Luke Agrippa from becoming Judge Biggs; to stop the murder; and to figure out how to get home before my time ran out. I had no idea how I'd know when my time was almost out, but I figured there would be some kind of sign. I sure hoped so.

"Man, are you lucky I'm around to remember stuff like it's cold in late October," said Charlie. "I couldn't find a coat that looked right, but I found this."

He tossed me a thick brown cardigan sweater, Irish looking, with leather-covered buttons. It reeked of mothballs.

"Well, at least I can cross 'killer moth attacks' off my list of concerns," I said.

"You're welcome," said Charlie.

As we walked to The Octagon, Charlie asked me if I wanted him to stay, just sort of hang out on The Octagon until I vanished and came back or whatever I was going to do, which was a nice thing to ask, and even though I really, really, really wanted him to, I said no.

"I'm supposed to let go of everything but the stars and the date and not think about anything that might tie me to the here and now. If you were right there, well, I might think about— I mean, I might have trouble— It might make me want to—"

Good grief. I told myself that I had to be pretty darn nervous to be suddenly getting all awkward and girlie about Charlie. Stammering? *Blushing?*

"I get it," Charlie said, quickly. "It's cool. But you come find me the second you get back and tell me what happened. Or else. By the way, how long do you think you'll be gone? And will you, like, disappear?"

"I don't think so, because the way I understand it, it'll

take no time at all," I said. "None of *our* time, that is. I mean, I guess it'll take a while for me to get into the trance or whatever and go through the portal into 1938, but once I'm there, I'll be using up 1938 time, not our time."

"So no matter how long you're in the past, you'll come back to the exact same moment in 2014 that you left?"

"Yeah. Does that sound right?"

Charlie grinned. "Well, except for the fact that all of this sounds totally insane, sure! Exactly right."

When we got to The Octagon, there was no big, serious good-bye. Charlie held out his fist, and we bumped knuckles.

"Good luck," he said. "Don't do anything stupid."

"Thanks for the advice," I said. "Very helpful."

He grinned an evil grin and walked backward a few steps, his hands shoved into his pockets then he turned around and jogged across the grass. When I couldn't see him anymore, I lay down on The Octagon, pulled the smelly sweater tightly around me, and began.

"October 26, 1938," I whispered.

I don't know how long it took, maybe hours, maybe minutes. All I know is that the boards of The Octagon stopped pressing against my back, and I stopped feeling chilly and became very light—weightless and floating— and the date I was going to stopped being a chant—*October 26, 1938; October 26, 1938*—and became a song I sang effortlessly and with my entire self, and it was beautiful.

And then I was in this pearly-light-soaked place, if you could call it a place since it didn't somehow feel located anywhere, and so was maybe more like a state, a sort of perfect, suspended balance of peace and shine, and then the portals started quietly blooming around me, shimmering and opening, shimmering and shutting, and I wasn't nervous about finding the right one, even though you would think I might have been. And then one opened in front of me and just a little to the left, and I knew it was the one, and I didn't step into it, just leaned toward it, so slightly, and was—through.

Then: pain and noise and images. Pain that was like being squeezed one second and yanked by every limb the next. Noise that was the October 26-song turned into a tornado roar and a drawn-out scream. Images that were ordinary and horrible and heartbreaking and pretty: a dying horse, its eyes full of terror; clothes flapping on a line; a boy no older than Charlie shooting someone; a man in a black suit sobbing with his head in his hands; a girl in a skirt, spinning; a house on fire; a boy playing a violin; a mother rocking her baby; something dead, covered in flies. Everything whirling faster and faster, the song a bright knife through my head, pain and more pain.

I swear I could feel it: history resisting.

Then: wooden boards pressing into my shoulder

blades, my body one long ache. I opened my eyes to darkness that became a whitish sky that became a white ceiling that became the white-painted inside of a peaked roof, eight triangles leaning in toward each other. *Eight*, I thought, *eight*. A gazebo roof. The Octagon, back before it was mine and Charlie's.

I lay there, staring at that ceiling, breathing hard, too scared to move, and then, after a while, because I didn't know what else to do, I sat up, stood up, and started walking.

CHAPTER TEN

Josh
1938

THE PRESIDENT, OWNER, AND chief executive officer
of Victory Fuels, the great Theodore K. Ratliff, saw that
picture of Preston in the *Times*. And I've always believed
Preston's picture is what turned the tide in our favor.
Aristotle had already gotten old Mr. Ratliff to take note of
our plight, to answer a few of our letters, to start asking
questions about how Biggs treated us, and to think about us
as people, not just mine machinery. As soon as Ratliff came
across my little brother playing taps in the paper, he ordered
his personal railroad car attached to the Desert Zephyr,
and he sent a telegram to Aristotle saying he was headed
for Victory with a contract in his briefcase, an agreement
guaranteeing fair wages and safe working conditions. The
citizens of Canvasburg unanimously elected Aristotle to
sign it for us all when Mr. Ratliff arrived.

We'd won.

The morning of the day Mr. Ratliff's train was scheduled to arrive, I made breakfast as usual. I wasn't too good at it, but I was the only one in the family whose body parts all worked. I was excited because I had a half dozen oranges for Preston. I'd earned them by hiking three miles south to an orange grove and working half a day digging irrigation ditches. People were starting to claim oranges had a magic ingredient called vitamin C. Made you healthy. I figured even though Doc O'Malley had sprung Preston from the infirmary and he was on the mend again, he still needed all the vitamin C he could get.

And I baked biscuits with flour mailed from Salt Lake City. Baked them for, I don't know, a good half hour at least.

Not much later, as I sat in the doorway of our tent scraping the ashes off the biscuits—or, as Preston liked to call them, meteorites—I watched the first sunlight of the day boiling over the desert like a tide of red rolling up to drown me. I held my breath, as if that would save me, but I couldn't go without air forever, and as I breathed again, a ruby crescent peeked over the rim of the world. In seconds, it had grown into a scarlet crown; then it was half an orange globe, and then a yellow ball, huge, glued to the horizon, and *thwock*, the ball pulled itself loose and floated up into the blue sky, burning whiter as it rose.

Suddenly, I spied a girl. I'd never seen this girl before. I'd never seen a girl *like* this girl before, flitting from tent shadow to tent shadow. She had hair as red as the sunlight that'd just singed my retinas. She had eyes so green, I could see them fifty yards away, and her feet were really large.

"You gonna bring those meteorites in or write a poem about 'em?" demanded Preston, sticking his head out of the tent.

I jumped a foot. And just like that, the girl was gone.

As I set the biscuits on the kitchen table, I heard Aristotle sing out "Ta-daaa!" like a Ringling Brothers ringmaster. Luke followed him into our tent. Some kind of optical illusion made it appear that their hair was short, neat, and slicked down on top of their skulls. Aristotle wore a jacket he must've managed to borrow from another miner—the sleeves were only a few inches too short. In his pocket was a neatly folded black-and-red handkerchief.

"Sharp—right down to the pocket square!" commented Mom.

Aristotle adjusted it slightly. "My talisman," he said proudly.

"What happened to your heads?" asked Preston.

"Wait—" gasped my dad. "You got haircuts?"

"I thought I heard a chainsaw," threw in Preston.

"For the big day," said Aristotle, patting him on the shoulder. "For the big meeting with Mr. Ratliff! We gonna get a safety inspector and a new elevator and time off when we hurt and a nine-hour workday and only five hours on Saturday and—"

Luke interrupted, caught up in the excitement. "And they say Biggs is gonna *get* it when Mr. Ratliff gets here! And US marshals are gonna track down those guys from the tank! And oh, brother, when they do!" Luke smacked his fist into his palm enthusiastically. And then he seemed to realize how worked up he'd let himself get and narrowed his eyes doubtfully. "Unless this is all one big joke and Mr. Ratliff and Biggs are just pulling our legs for a gas." He shot a level stare at Aristotle as if they'd discussed this angle already, but his father didn't seem to notice.

It wasn't easy being Luke. Proud of his dad and angry at him all at the same time.

"Hey—you guys—come look! The detectives are gone!" shouted Preston from the door of the tent.

"Great day in the morning!" said my dad, rolling my mom outside. "Let's have a look." Before I could follow, Aristotle grabbed my shoulder.

"Josh," he said quietly, "I think this is gonna go good. But"—and for a second, his optimism, his hope, his confidence, the things he wore like armor every day of his life, dropped away—"you never know."

"Aristotle—" I said.

"However it happens—you're Luke's friend. And that

boy, he love two things. He love what is right. And he love to win. And I don't know which he love more. If I'm not around, you help him choose, Josh."

"If you're not around? Are you planning a trip? Are you headed for Hawaii?" I asked, taking a wild stab at a joke because Aristotle sounded so serious, it scared me.

But Aristotle had already stepped into the sunshine. I followed.

Down by Honey Brook, there was the girl again.

"Who *is* that?" I muttered.

"Who is what?" asked Aristotle.

"That girl," I said, pointing.

"What girl?" asked Aristotle.

She was gone.

"You getting too worked up, Josh," said Aristotle. "You seeing things."

The crowd began gathering three hours before Mr. Ratliff arrived. Preston had put together a combo with a few kids from school, and they kicked off on the platform of the railroad station sometime around two. My parents sat in the front row to listen, and Luke was already there with his dad. I'd told them all to go on without me—I'd lost something and needed to find it. I didn't tell them I was searching for a girl, possibly imaginary, who disappeared whenever anybody besides me looked at her.

I thought maybe I was bats. It was like I'd spotted one of those ghosts that disintegrate when the sun rises. I glanced around camp, but no dice; just the Spanakopolouses rinsing out their socks for the big event. Mr. Ratliff's train whistle wailed out there on the desert, so I had to give up.

I couldn't work my way through the crowd to Luke. The mob surged and I got close to the front, but then it flowed backward and pulled me away. About all I could make out was the sight of Dad studying Mom's tires nervously.

A little girl standing near me, a little blond town girl in a dress that cost more than any dress my mom had ever owned, kept eyeing me. Finally, she yanked loose from her mother, marched up to me, planted both feet on the dusty ground, and declared: "My mother says you should be *thanking* us. Instead of bothering poor Mr. Ratliff. My mom says we *gave* you jobs, and all you could do was complain, when you should say thank you. And now *nobody's* making any money! *My* mom says people like you, what are you good for! My mom says she hopes you're happy, you upset that nice old man in his house and he had to come from New York!"

Before I could give the little angel my opinion of all this, I saw the red-haired girl again, from the corner of my eye, shimmering like a mirage on the far edge of the crowd, shamrock-green eyes on me for a second and then flashing somewhere else. Those eyes were like being zapped by the tail of a South American eel.

"Nice talking to you," I said to the sweetie pie, "but I gotta scamper."

I thought about fighting my way to the front to tell Luke about the red-haired girl haunting our town, but what was I going to say? "There's a girl here! And she's got red hair! And green eyes! And nobody seems to notice her but me!" Instead, I decided it would be better to catch her first and then tell people about her, so I scuttled around the crowd and began searching again.

Mr. Ratliff's train was still a good ten minutes away. Victory was only three blocks long and four blocks wide, so I had time. I gazed up A Street and B Street, and when there was only C Street left, I glanced down an alleyway and spied her slipping up the back stairs of the Victory Fuels Corporation headquarters. Since I only saw her climb as high as the second floor, I figured she'd either managed to slip inside or she was hunkered down on the landing, hoping I hadn't spotted her. Up the steps I clambered.

I found her crouched on the corrugated iron, calmly staring at me over the top step. When I skidded to a stop to keep from tripping over her, she gave a smile as if, somehow, she already knew me.

"Caught you!" was all I could come up with.

"Because I let you," she returned.

"What?" I asked.

"I had to talk to you. But only you. I had to let *you* catch me, and nobody else," she said.

"That's what the disappearing act was all about?" I asked.

She nodded.

"Hold on. Are you," I began, finally putting two and two together about the green eyes, "Doc O'Malley's— niece?" I asked.

"That's a long story," she sighed. She stood and glanced up and down the alley.

"*What* story is a long story?" I asked. "Who are you?"

"Margaret O'Malley," she said.

"I *knew* it," I said, offering my hand. "An O'Malley. I'm Josh. Josh Garrett."

"Of course you are," she replied, shaking my hand firmly. "And—and—I'm sorry. But there's something I have to tell you."

Margaret was the first O'Malley I'd ever met who didn't have glasses as thick as the window of a submarine in a novel by Jules Verne. I was afraid her eyes might fry me to a crisp.

At that moment, a cheer went up from across town, which meant Mr. Ratliff's arrival had happened, and I'd missed it, but I didn't mind too much because his big meeting with Aristotle was the next day, and our moment in the sun was still coming, and in the meantime, this Margaret O'Malley was turning out to be very interesting.

Without wasting energy on further introductions, she launched into a story about traveling through time that was so strange, improbable, eerie, sad, infuriating, and confusing, and at the same time so incredibly similar to Aunt Bridey's, that I had no choice but to believe every word. She left the details hazy enough so that when the future arrived, I wouldn't be able to get myself into too much trouble, but the upshot was, history as she understood it showed that Elijah Biggs was destined to murder Theodore Ratliff the next day and frame Aristotle Agrippa for the crime.

"But there's no way Elijah Biggs would do something like that," I objected when she was done. "Sure. He's awful. And he has it in for Aristotle Agrippa. But he wouldn't kill his boss. I mean, if Mr. Ratliff were dead, who would be president of Victory Fuels International?"

Margaret stared patiently at me.

"Oh," I said. "Right. Elijah Biggs would."

"It's absolutely true. Mr. Ratliff will die tomorrow unless I do something," she said.

"Unless *we* do something," I corrected. "Come on. We have to find Luke."

"No," said Margaret, stopping dead. "He can't know I'm here. Nobody can know I'm here. No police, no bodyguards, no friends or brothers or dads or moms, and especially no Luke Agrippa. I can't let anybody know what I'm up to. I have to keep my effect on history as tiny as possible."

"Then why'd you tell me?" I asked.

"Because I know you," replied Margaret, "even if you don't know me. And because I can't do this alone."

"Well, we *have* to tell Luke," I insisted. "He's smarter than I am. And taller. And can throw things farther."

"What kind of things?" asked Margaret.

"For instance a football," I said.

"How far?" she asked.

"At least forty-five yards," I said. "Some people say fifty."

"Well, that's impressive," said Margaret, "but we're still leaving him out of it."

"Then I'm taking you to see Aunt Bridey," I finally said, ducking behind the fence along C Street, which was the only way to get to the foot of Mount Hosta without being seen. "I don't care if you want to or not."

"Aunt Bridey?" asked Margaret uncertainly, as if she recognized the name.

"If Elijah Biggs really has it in for Mr. Ratliff, and we're going to have a snowball's chance in July of stopping him, then we have to ask Aunt Bridey for help," I told Margaret, turning toward the mountain, "because I don't have a clue about what to do next, and if anybody does, she does, and that's just how it is."

"My dad used to tell stories about his aunt Bridey," mused Margaret.

"What did he say?" I asked.

"She was a moonshiner."

"Then his stories were true," I replied.

CHAPTER ELEVEN

Margaret
1938

AUNT BRIDEY HAD THE O'MALLEY eyes, all right, as I had plenty of opportunity to observe, since the second she opened her door to find us standing there, she jutted her head forward and slapped a stare on me so hard, I stumbled backward and just about fell.

"You hold still!" she snapped.

I obeyed. Then she whipped off her glasses, hunched to get eye level with me, and stared some more before she whipped her glasses back on (turns out it's possible to do this) and eyed me head to toe, using those thick lenses like a Cub Scout uses a magnifying glass to focus sunshine on a bug and fry it.

"Giiirrll," said Aunt Bridey, shaking her head and stretching out the word like chewing gum, "I'm in the middle of pickling okra! This had *better* be good."

"It is," said Joshua, quickly.

"I *mean*," said Aunt Bridey, ignoring him completely and narrowing her eyes at me, "if you just did what I think you just did, then somebody better be about to *die*!"

"How about three people?" I blurted out. "Would three people be enough? Two in 1938 and one in 2014?"

"And here I was," sighed Aunt Bridey, raising her eyes imploringly to the sky, "thinking I was done hearing my relatives say things like that." She gathered herself together. "Except I guess the only relative who said them was me. All right. Sit down. Tell me who."

At Aunt Bridey's kitchen table, I said, "Theodore Ratliff."

"Now? In my time?" asked Aunt Bridey. "In 1938?"

"Yes," I replied. "Tomorrow night."

"Who else?"

I swallowed and glanced at Josh, who would be hearing this part for the first time.

"Nobody, if we save Ratliff," I said. "But if we don't . . . Aristotle Agrippa."

Josh shot me a stunned look.

"What? Why?" he asked.

"And who," pressed Aunt Bridey, ignoring Josh, "in 2014?"

So far, I hadn't mentioned my dad to Josh either, figuring that the less he knew about a future he'd one day be walking around in, the better. But since he was in this with me, it seemed only fair to give him at least a bare-minimum, no-details idea of what was at stake. I took a breath.

"My father," I said.

Joshua opened his mouth probably to ask questions, but then shut it, which I appreciated.

"I think he'll be . . . your great-nephew, when he's born, in 1968," I told Aunt Bridey.

"You'd better give me the whole story," she sighed, turning off the fire beneath her pot of okra with a shrug of resignation.

"You know I can't give you the whole story," I said.

"Tell me what you can," instructed Aunt Bridey.

So I told her about Elijah Biggs's dirty, double-crossing ways, about the murder of Theodore Ratliff and the faked suicide-murder of Aristotle at the infirmary, and how these awful things would lead to other awful things that I couldn't tell her and Josh about, which would lead to my father's life being in terrible danger in ways that I also couldn't tell her and Josh about.

"But some of the things have to do with Luke," I said, looking right at Josh.

"You mean Luke's in danger?" said Josh, his eyes widening.

I nodded.

"If we save Ratliff, we save Aristotle; if we save Aristotle, we save Luke," I said, simply.

"Save Luke's life?" asked Josh.

I considered saying yes and leaving it at that, but when I saw the fear on Josh's face, I just couldn't. Luke was his best friend, I reminded myself, just the same way Charlie was mine.

"Save him from the life he'll lead if we don't save his dad, and believe me when I say he really, really needs to get saved from that."

Aunt Bridey zapped me with a glare. "What if you don't stop Ratliff's murder? Because history doesn't want to change, you know. History resists. If you don't stop Ratliff's murder tomorrow, what will you do?" she asked. "Give up and go home?"

I swallowed hard. "No. I—I'll think of something."

"Because I wonder if you realize how little time you have?"

"*How* little, um, exactly?"

"Three days was the longest I could ever stick it out."

I felt like someone had thrown a bucket of ice water over my head. *Three days.* I'd hoped for at least a week.

"Family legend has it that one of our ancestors eked out five, but I have my doubts. You look strong enough, even if you're on the skinny side, but no human being's stronger than history when it's resisting."

"How will I know when it's time to leave?"

"You'll know. Your own body will tell you, and by gum, you'd better listen to it when it does!"

"Why?" asked Josh. "What will happen if she stays too long?"

"I only know what I've been told, but I believe it," said Aunt Bridey. "She'll die, right here in 1938 *and* in her own time, too, I guess, since she'll never get back to it. Or worse will happen."

"Worse than *dying*?" I asked.

"Well, I guess that depends on your perspective, but finding yourself wedged between dimensions with numbers higher than either of us could count to, stuck forever outside of time and space, sounds worse to me."

I shivered. But *three days*? It might be just enough time, if everything went according to plan, but since I didn't have a plan yet, much less a backup plan, the idea of three days was sending me right to the edge of panic.

"So I'll go home and come back!" I cried out. "If I need more time."

But Aunt Bridey was shaking her head.

"I tried that, but it takes a long time for your mind and body to get strong enough to defy history and travel again. A year, in my case, give or take."

"But in a year, my father could be—"

I covered my face with my hands.

"I'm sorry, Margaret," said Aunt Bridey, her voice suddenly heavy with sadness, "but it's better that I tell you these things than that you find out the hard way."

I uncovered my face and looked at Aunt Bridey, who was staring over my head, possibly out of the kitchen window, possibly into the distant, distant past.

"Learn the hard way," I said, softly, "like you did?"

"I made so many blunders," lamented Aunt Bridey. "The biggest one was attempting anything at all. But you've already made that one, and there's no going back. The second one was falling in love."

"With Lieutenant Walker?" asked Josh. "The Confederate soldier from your photo?"

"With him and with his cause."

"You mean the rebel cause? Slavery? Breaking up the union?" I asked.

Aunt Bridey snorted. "Of course not. He was a deserter. Tried to leave that ugliness behind and start what he called a utopian society right here in Victory. No slaves, everyone working together. Came darn close, too, but his past caught up with him. I wanted so much to save him, maybe even could have, but . . ."

"But what?"

Aunt Bridey snapped to, dropped her sad, misty look like a hot potato, and said, matter-of-factly, "Your eyes are going to go bad. By the time you're eighteen, you won't see the portals opening, not even with glasses, not with anything. By the time you're eighteen, you're done."

She stood up, slapped her hands on her apron, and went back to her okra.

"You couldn't go back when you most needed to, could you?" I said. "You needed to travel one last time, but your time ran out, your eyes got weak, you didn't know it would happen, and Lieutenant Walker——"

She stirred that okra as if her life depended on it.

"I let him down," she said, flatly.

It turned out that even after she couldn't time travel anymore, Aunt Bridey didn't lose her adventurous spirit. Once she'd recovered, as much as she'd ever recover, from the Lieutenant Walker heartbreak, she'd done a lot of things in her life before she moved back to the house on Mount Hosta to grow her garden and tend her bees. One of them was ride the Desert Zephyr to Los Angeles to work in the movies. Because of her glasses, Aunt Bridey didn't end up onscreen. She became a makeup artist, and she turned out to be a big help in hatching our plot to infiltrate Mr. Ratliff's hunting lodge to save his life.

It wasn't too much trouble for Aunt Bridey to give Josh sideburns, wrinkles, a bald spot, and a nose the size of W. C. Fields's. Then she proceeded to dye my hair the color of dirt, coil it like a big cinnamon bun at the back of my head, plaster me with makeup, and—glory of glories—strap a giant fake butt made of goose down under my maid's outfit.

As it turned out, Aunt Bridey, always full of surprises, had been earning a good-sized pile of money every year by supplying fancy-pants gourmet fruit, vegetables, spices, jam, and honey to Mr. Ratliff's mountain hunting lodge. His cook, Mrs. Orilla, had just placed an order of goodies for Mr. Ratliff to gorge on during his visit to Victory.

"Mrs'. Orilla will get a couple of unexpected vegetables in her order," said Aunt Bridey, with a wink at me and Josh.

Eyeing my mind-boggling rump, Josh muttered, "More like an extra load of watermelons."

Of course, I had no choice but to kick him. Kicking isn't easy when you're shaped the way I now was, but I managed.

The hunting lodge was just a few miles up the side of Mount Hosta, but the donkey path was so steep and rocky that even without my new encumbrance, it would've been hard going. Nevertheless, Aunt Bridey loaded her donkey with provisions and marched us straight up that mountain, mentioning, on the way, the layout of Mr. Ratliff's lodge, including the system of dumbwaiters linking the rooms to his basement kitchen. When we arrived, she forced Mrs. Orilla to hire us as extra staff during Mr. Ratliff's stay. I didn't understand all the conversation, which was mostly in Spanish, but it seemed to involve the cook saying no, and Aunt Bridey telling her good luck fixing Mr. Ratliff's dinner when all the provisions she'd ordered mysteriously fell off the burro and tumbled down the mountain, not to mention the three bottles of Honey Brook Nectar Mr. Ratliff adored so much.

"*Mañana*, three p.m.," snapped Mrs. Orilla at me and Josh. "Mr. Ratliff arrives at five."

We labored back down the mountain to Aunt Bridey's house, and Josh put the donkey away in his little barn. Then Aunt Bridey turned, stuck a hand on her hip, and pointed at us.

"It's up to you, now," she said.

CHAPTER TWELVE

Josh
1938

"MR. RATLIFF'S ALMOST HERE!" came the whisper down the line.

"He hasn't even started up the mountain!" came the next.

"He's in the yard!"

"He walks with a cane now. It'll be hours."

"He went to visit the people in Canvasburg."

"His bodyguard, Earl, keeps stopping to smoke."

"He's on the porch."

"He's spending the night on his train."

"The meeting is postponed."

"The meeting is canceled."

"Mr. Ratliff was never really coming at all."

The rumors kept swirling down the row of servants assembled in the hallway of Theodore K. Ratliff's famous mountain lodge. Margaret and I had done everything we could think of to prepare for the events to come, and all we could do now was stand there with everybody else and wait.

We'd reported for work two hours before, armed with a very simple plan: stop the murder. Even if we'd had time to think of something better, I don't know what we'd have come up with, because we didn't know anything about what was going to happen except that it *had* happened—in the cigar parlor on the top floor of Mr. Ratliff's lodge. Yes. This was the kind of hunting lodge that came complete with a cigar parlor.

So for two hours, along with an army of maids, messengers, butlers, waiters, and gardeners, we helped prepare Mr. Ratliff's digs for his arrival. His lodge was like something in a movie, gleaming, glimmering, gilded, burnished, bronzed, lacquered, layered, waxed, varnished, and spectacular, hidden up there amid the mountain ridges. Once, when I was little, my parents had led Preston and me into the Peabody Hotel in Memphis, Tennessee, to show us the mahogany tables, Tiffany glass, leather chairs, crystal decanters, and gold-plated boxes for keeping cigars in called "humidors." I'm telling you what, that place had nothing on Mr. Ratliff's lodge, except maybe the family of ducks swimming in the fountain.

Margaret's job was to dust the antlers of all the animals

Mr. Ratliff had shot over the years.

Me, they handed a bottle of furniture polish and sent into the parlor. There I stood, all alone in the room where it would happen, which might have been a stroke of luck, if I'd had any idea *what* was going to happen. On a giant oak desk sat a crystal paperweight big enough to crack a skull wide open, so I hid that behind a fern. I stashed a stray letter opener in the roots of a potted rubber tree. There was also a pen on the desk, heavier than lead. As I read the tiny gold letters along the cap (MATTERHORN: 24 K GOLD) something caught my eye in the corner of the room: a dumbwaiter. Judging from the aroma of roasting duck wafting out of it, I was pretty sure it led to the kitchen. Smoking cigars must've whetted Mr. Ratliff's appetite. I wedged the dumbwaiter door open a hair, not enough to notice from inside the room, but enough to keep it from latching. At the bottom of the shaft, I could hear Margaret talking the cook into letting her keep Mr. Ratliff's glass full during the meeting. The voices died out.

"Put it down, boy!" shrieked a voice from the doorway. I spun around to see Mrs. Orilla with her hands on her hips. "Don't you get any ideas!" she snarled. I realized I still had that blasted Matterhorn pen in my hand, and I ditched it on the desktop pronto, shooting her an innocent smile. If that old lady had had any inkling what I actually *did* have in my mind, her hair would've fallen out on the spot. "Get out here in the hall and wait at attention with the rest of us!"

So I went to stand in line to listen to the rumors fly, and the wait dragged on. For some reason, I couldn't stop thinking about that pen. I knew Mr. Ratliff was one of the good guys. But his pen—that one fountain pen, which lay all year on a desk in a hunting lodge collecting dust and got used maybe five days out of every three hundred and sixty-five, that one neglected solid gold toy cost enough to feed all of Canvasburg for a year. The lodge itself—the money sunk into that place would've fixed everything that was wrong in the lives of everybody I had ever known—forever—and I just had to wonder—

—and of course, as soon as my mind had drifted so far down this road that I almost had it in me to ask if Mr. Ratliff, white beard, pink cheeks, good intentions, and all, didn't have a thing or two to answer for himself, all heck broke loose.

"Mr. Ratliff's here!" shouted the butler from the front porch. "Mr. Biggs is here! Cue the quartet!"

And I'll be a monkey's uncle if there wasn't an entire string quartet socked away in a corner that I had completely missed. The violins, viola, and cello launched into a song that called to mind a platoon of dukes in buckle shoes sashaying around a ballroom with their duchesses.

"Ah, Aristotle, welcome to my home away from home!" cried Mr. Theodore Ratliff as he swept through the front door, Aristotle Agrippa half a step behind, and Elijah Biggs bringing up the rear, coated in dust cut through with little arroyos of sweat. "You've convinced me, sir. Your ideas are fascinating. We'll add them to the agreement right now. In addition to a living wage and safe working conditions, the Victory Corporation will also provide medical care at a fully equipped hospital. And fund a library. And endow a scholarship fund for the children! What's good for the people is good for the company!" He twirled his walking cane. Biggs scowled.

To the assembled staff, Mr. Ratliff said, "At ease! Take a break! Earl, for heaven's sake, go outside and have yourself a cigarette. My new friend and I will be in the parlor. Mrs. Orilla, please send up my Honey Brook Nectar in short order." And with that, he led Aristotle and Biggs upstairs.

Margaret ran for the kitchen to grab the nectar for Mr. Ratliff, and I followed her, slipping into the massive kitchen. I caught her eye as she hurried past. "Good luck," I whispered.

"Don't worry," she assured me, and while Mrs. Orilla described the terrible fate destined to befall any worker who spilled moonshine on Mr. Ratliff's trousers, I climbed into the dumbwaiter, latched the hatch, and hauled on the rope.

The dumbwaiter wouldn't budge.

I tried again, but even with all my weight hanging on

the rope, nothing happened.

History resists.

Through the shaft above me, I could hear their voices.

". . . little memento," I heard Aristotle saying. "Thank you."

"And now I propose a toast," boomed Mr. Ratliff. "To Aristotle Agrippa. To the little boy in the newspaper. To the miners and their families. To an old man whose eyes have been opened!"

I heard the door creak, and I heard footsteps cross the floor. Margaret. Crystal clinked. Honey Brook Nectar gurgled from the bottle.

"To the future!" declared Mr. Ratliff. "Drink up!"

"I," said Elijah Biggs distinctly, "refuse."

"Drink the toast, Elijah," said Mr. Ratliff. "So we can sign Aristotle's agreement and change a few hundred lives for the better." After a pause, he said it again. "Drink. Drink!"

"It's all well and good," came Biggs's voice, finally, "for you to sit here on your mountain and play Santa Claus, giving away presents to every little miner who asks for something. Money, safety equipment, hospitals, libraries, scholarships, holidays, vacations. Well, bully for you. You got rich a long time ago. Now I'm the one who has to run the mine, I'm the one who has to make money, and if we start treating these dirty scum like people, and they get the idea they have rights, then my profits go up in smoke."

"I ordered you to toast Aristotle Agrippa," replied Mr. Ratliff stiffly.

"Toast Agrippa?" scoffed Biggs. "People like him are different from you and me. You can't reason with them. You can't talk to them. And you certainly don't drink toasts to them. One day I'm going to be in charge of this company, and when I am, the last thing I need is a bunch of miners who think they have rights—"

"Unless you toast Aristotle Agrippa this second," said Mr. Ratliff, "and do exactly as I say when it comes to the workers of Victory Fuels, that day might not come at all."

"What are you saying?" asked Biggs.

"I'm saying toast Aristotle Agrippa," replied Mr. Ratliff in a voice that left no doubt how he'd become the president of one of the largest companies on earth. "Now."

"Mr. Ratliff," began Aristotle, "there's no need."

"I think there is, though," said Mr. Ratliff. "Elijah. We're waiting."

I heard a chair scrape across the floor. I heard it fall against the door of the shaft above me.

"Stop him!" cried Margaret. "He's going to kill Mr. Ratliff!"

"Ridiculous!" said Mr. Ratliff. "He'll do exactly as I say. Elijah? What are you—"

And there I sat, stuck in the dumbwaiter. Desperate, I

balled up my fists and punched the top until it splintered. Hand over hand, I climbed the shaft, but when I got to the top, the door opened three-quarters of an inch and jammed. Biggs's chair had wedged against it. I was trapped in the shaft, hanging by my fingernails.

Through the crack in the door, I spied Mr. Ratliff frozen at his desk, clutching Aristotle's favorite old Greek pen in his hand. Biggs lumbered slowly toward him, his face dead blank, holding the gold Matterhorn pen like— like a dagger.

"Mr. Ratliff! Watch youself! I think he's really gonna—" shouted Aristotle, leaping to his feet.

But before he could grasp what was happening, Margaret sprang in front of Biggs, brandishing the crystal decanter of Honey Brook Nectar. And I swear, as sure as my name is Josh Garrett, the bearskin rug on Mr. Ratliff's floor turned its head one sixty-fourth of an inch and snagged the heel of her large shoe with its teeth. She fell, and the bottle of nectar shattered, filling the room with a sharp, sweet odor.

History resists.

As Biggs stepped over her, Aristotle managed to grab him from behind, clamping down with all his strength while Biggs thrashed like a wolverine in a trap.

"Elijah," snapped Mr. Ratliff, standing. "Get hold of yourself!"

"I'm done taking orders from you, old man!" snarled Biggs.

Margaret lay on the floor, dazed, struggling to regain her feet. And slowly Aristotle, strong as he was, lost his grip on Elijah Biggs. Greed. Rage. Hatred. Through a crack in a small doorway, I witnessed the precise moment when Biggs broke free.

"I don't understand!" cried Mr. Ratliff.

I wedged my feet in the corners of the dumbwaiter shaft and shoved against the door with everything I had. It gave. I tumbled through and ran straight at Biggs, colliding with him halfway across the room. Maybe I should've gone out for the football team after all.

Biggs dropped the pen and struggled to focus his dazed eyes on me, but God bless Aunt Bridey, she'd glued my makeup on so tight, it would've stuck to a Hollywood stuntman diving off a runaway stagecoach. He didn't know who I was.

I wrapped my arms around his knees and held on for all I was worth. It was like clutching a cornered grizzly bear. A mindless, black rage. He shook me off like a German shepherd shaking off his bath and snatched the gold pen from the floor.

Aristotle came swooping through the air to take it.

Half a second late.

Biggs plunged his weapon straight into the neck of old

Mr. Ratliff, who began dying that second, taking all our hopes and all our futures with him.

And now Biggs had more evil to accomplish. He grabbed Mr. Ratliff's ebony cane. Leaping sideways, he caught Aristotle square in the belly, doubling him over. Margaret almost seemed to know what was coming next. As Biggs raised the cane over his head to bring it down on the back of Aristotle's skull, she started to lunge between them, but history did it again—the slick pool of spilled nectar sent her tumbling head over heels.

The cane descended with a nauseating crunch on the back of Aristotle's skull. He dropped like a sack of flour. "Aristotle!" I cried, afraid he was dead. "Aristotle! Please!"

Elijah Biggs lifted the cane to deliver the fatal blow, but I managed to leap up and grab it from behind. Margaret scrabbled across the floor to shield Aristotle with her body. I realized that Biggs wouldn't stop until he'd killed us all. I didn't know whether he'd been planning to kill Mr. Ratliff all along or if he'd done it on impulse, but now that he had, his way forward was clear: we were witnesses. Alive, we could put him in the electric chair. Dead, we'd leave the path to the presidency of Victory Fuels wide open.

I tried to yank the cane away from him, but he was a cyclone of pure anger, and as for me—he would have to kill me before I let him hurt Margaret.

Frantic footsteps sounded outside the cigar parlor.

"Mr. Ratliff! Mr. Ratliff! Mr. Ratliff!" cried Mrs. Orilla from the hallway, rattling the door that Biggs must've locked behind them. "What's happening?"

CHAPTER THIRTEEN

Margaret
1938

FOR A SECOND, THINGS GOT BLURRY, and the horrible noise of that cane against Aristotle's head seemed to echo in my ears. My flailing hand found the edge of a table, and I yanked myself to my feet in time to see Biggs whirl around and clamber, caveman-like, his face bloated with rage, dragging a chair behind him toward the quaking door to wedge it tight so he could finish us off. I caught sight of Mr. Ratliff, and that's when things got clear and real, way too real: his once slicked-back hair unstuck and falling in strings on his forehead, his face slack, his blue eyes blank and glassy like raw oysters, and blood, syrupy, brutally red, and smelling—I swear I could smell it—like pennies, soaking his white shirt. And there was Aristotle. Oh, Aristotle. He was real, too, and so human it could crack your heart in two.

I didn't mean to say it, to make the promise I made. But somehow, when I looked down at Aristotle, white as death, but so brave, decent, and dad-like, I wanted like crazy to give him something. My first idea was to put all that precious blood that was pouring out of his head and onto the shiny wood floor back where it belonged, but that was impossible, and there wasn't even time to try to stanch his wound. So what I did instead was cross my heart hard and say, "We'll save Luke, Mr. Agrippa. I swear to you we will."

And then I noticed his handkerchief and pen—the one not made of gold—lying next to him, and even though Biggs had turned and was striding toward me across the room, snarling like a mad dog, the black cane slicing the air, and even though Josh had jumped between us, his arms thrown out, and was shouting, "Run! *Now!*" I couldn't stand the thought of Aristotle's poor, ordinary personal belongings getting scooped up by Biggs or one of his minions and thrown away like nothing, so I stopped to scoop them up myself.

Then Josh was grabbing my hand, yanking me up, and we were bursting through the French doors to the balcony and then shimmying down a tree to the ground, and running, running, running, running till our lungs crackled and our hearts were about to jump straight out of our chests, running, running through the cool night air.

After what felt like forever, Josh pulled me down behind a big stand of shrubs and said, "Shhh."

We crouched there, listening for shouting or footsteps. My held breath clawed at the inside of my chest like a caged animal. When we didn't hear anything, we both fell backward onto the ground with a *thunk* and just lay there, panting, until our nerves, hearts, and lungs had settled down. More or less. In my case, less. I was pretty sure my entire body would never feel normal again.

We rested for a minute; then, slowly, we got up and started walking, but after a few yards, I saw stars in front of my eyes, grabbed my knees, and leaned over.

"You all right?" asked Josh.

"I don't know," I said hoarsely. "To tell you the truth, I feel kind of weird."

"We-ll," said Josh, slowly, "it's been a weird kind of a day."

Even upside down and in the dark, I could hear the dry note in his voice that meant he was grinning a half-sad, half-goofy grin, and somehow, that was just what I needed to hear. I stood up straight and grinned back.

"I hate to tell you this, but you seem to have lost your bald spot," I said.

He patted the top of his head, tugging at his hair.

"Shoot, it's a hair-growth miracle!"

Then he looked at me and laughed.

"You, on the other hand, seem to have hung on to your substantial, uh, caboose."

I reached around, slapped myself on the false rump, and said, "Yee-haw!" and—*wham*—we just flat-out lost it. Hooted. Howled. We grabbed our rib cages. Tears ran down our cheeks. We laughed so hard, we had to sit down, me on my padded caboose. At some point, Josh yanked off his fake nose and threw it into the trees, and we laughed harder. It sounds like we were acting crazy or disrespectful or something, but maybe this was how things were supposed to go: you saw the worst thing you've ever seen or imagined, a thing that made you feel a hundred years old and broken in a million places, and then you fell down on the ground laughing at the stupidest jokes like idiots or like the thirteen-year-old kids you were. Whether it was disrespectful or not, it sure felt good.

As our laughing turned sputtery, then hiccuppy, a thought struck me, knocking the last bit of laughter right out of me.

"Listen, listen!" I said, grabbing Josh's sleeve. "Maybe he'll blame *us* for the murder now. You know, the substitute kitchen help or whatever, since we were there this time!"

"What?"

"Think about it! Maybe we've saved Aristotle after all!"

Josh stared at me and then down at the ground, lowering his eyebrows in a way that was so exactly like what Charlie always did when he was pondering that it gave me a sharp twinge of homesickness.

"I hope so," he said, "but I don't think so."

"Why?"

"Remember what you told me. History is going to show that the point wasn't just to get rid of Ratliff and take over the company; the point was also to bring down Aristotle, so everyone would think he was a coward and would quit listening to him. If Aristotle were dead, *maybe* Biggs would've told people that two strangers attacked him and Mr. Ratliff, but since he's not . . ."

I sighed. "He needs to make it look like Aristotle got double-crossed by Ratliff, wimped out about going back down to Canvasburg a failure, asked for money to get away, and then killed Ratliff when he wouldn't give it to him."

"I guess that's about the size of it," said Josh. I heard him repeat the phrase "wimped out" under his breath, like he was trying it out for the first time, which I guess he probably was.

By the time we got to Aunt Bridey's, all the fresh, clean feeling the laughter had left was gone. When she opened the door, Aunt Bridey didn't say a word, just took one look at us, pulled us inside the house, and hugged us, first Josh, then me.

"Are you going to stand there all day? Sit down," she said at last. "I'll get you some tea."

"Turn around," I told Josh, and while his back was to me, I reached under my skirt and pulled off the false rump. I tossed it down, and when Josh got permission to turn back, he glanced at it lying there on the rug. Neither one of us laughed, just walked over and sat down on Aunt Bridey's stiff, embroidered sofa to wait.

I was halfway through my cup of tea when I started shaking, head to toe, uncontrollably, like I'd been taken over by my own personal earthquake. An image of Aristotle's stone-still, white face, the pool of blood widening under his cheek, kept appearing in my head. My hand trembled so that I spilled hot tea on my lap, but I didn't even feel it. Aunt Bridey gently took the cup from my hand and knelt beside me, her arms wrapping around me, warm and solid, but I kept shaking.

"History," I gasped. "History, history, history."

"I know," said Aunt Bridey. "Oh child, I know."

Sobs welled up from some deep place inside me, and suddenly, I was crying and I couldn't stop. It was like the horror of it all, of everything that had happened in the hunting lodge, fell on me all at once, like a big, smothering heap of coal dust.

"That man," I wailed, "that man was dead!"

Aunt Bridey just held on tighter and rocked me like a baby in her arms. I don't know how long we sat that way, me shaking and crying, her rocking and rocking, because eventually, I guess I fell asleep. When I woke up, I was in Aunt Bridey's spare-room bed, and morning light, lemonade colored and full of dancing dust, was beaming in through the curtains and across the heap of soft quilts that covered me.

For a few sweet seconds, I didn't remember a thing, just lay blinking into the light like a little kid. I gazed at the floating dust motes. I gazed at the flowered wallpaper and at the tall posts of the bed. Then I remembered.

"Josh!" I yelped, tossing off the quilts and swinging my legs over the edge of the bed.

"Stop!"

It was Aunt Bridey, tall in the doorway, her green eyes blazing. She carried a tray of food.

"But we have to save Aristotle!"

"Of course you do," she scoffed. "So it'd be a fine idea for you to jump out of bed and go tearing out of here to do it light-headed, weak, and without a thing in your stomach."

"I'm not weak!" I protested. "I'm not light-headed."

But even as I spoke the words, I realized that I was both of those things and a little short of breath, too. The room looked slightly fuzzy around the edges, and the roses on the wallpaper seemed to be swaying as though swept by a summer breeze. I pulled my legs back onto the bed, leaned against the headboard, and shut my eyes.

"Geez, I'm lame," I said.

"Lame? You hurt your leg last night?"

"No. At least, I don't think so, but since I seem to be a total idiotic wreck, who knows?"

Aunt Bridey set the tray, which held a pot of tea, a cup, and a breathtakingly big plate of eggs, toast, and bacon, on the table next to the bed.

"No, I just meant that first, I cry like a baby. Complete meltdown. Then I wake up all dizzy and trembly like an old lady with the flu. I just thought I was tougher than this."

Aunt Bridey handed me a cup of tea.

"Don't be foolish, girl. You *are* tougher than this. Drink."

I drank. I'd never been much of a tea drinker at home, but with that honey-gold tea of Aunt Bridey's running down my throat, I felt some of my strength come trickling back.

"Yeah, right," I said. "Josh must think I'm the biggest loser."

"He might think that," said Aunt Bridey sharply, "but not because of your behavior last night. I told him what I'll tell you: yes, the shock of the murder and your disappointment at not stopping it hit you hard, but mostly it was simple overstaying."

"What?"

Aunt Bridey took a hand mirror from the dresser behind her and held it up to my face.

"Look at your eyes. Glazed. Too big. Too bright. Like

a person with a fever, which you'll also likely get if you haven't already."

I blinked at my reflection, which had certainly seen better days. Aunt Bridey was right about my eyes. I was pale, too, and it wasn't only in contrast to my dyed mud-brown hair.

"It's time," said Aunt Bridey.

"Time for what?"

Aunt Bridey snorted impatiently.

"It's *time*. Our time, trying to push you out, send you on home where you belong. I told you that your body would know when it was time to go back. Well, it's starting to know. Now, eat."

I shoved in a forkful of eggs, bit off a corner of buttered toast. I wasn't about to admit it to bossy Aunt Bridey, but they both tasted as golden and delicious as the tea.

"But I can't leave before we save Aristotle," I protested, my mouth full.

Aunt Bridey shrugged.

"You have a little more time, but history doesn't like you much right now. The longer you stay, the sicker you'll get. Only way to keep it in check, as much as you can, is to eat plenty, drink plenty, especially good potent tea, and get sleep when you can. Pick that fork up, girl. Keep eating."

"I *am* eating," I said, crunching my way down a slice of bacon that tasted like greased heaven. "But I need to talk to Josh. We have to make a plan to break Aristotle out of that infirmary and get him out of town before, before—"

I couldn't say it.

"*Eat*. Josh left you a note about all that. When your plate's clean and that pot's empty, you can read it."

Under Aunt Bridey's watchful eye, I ate. And ate. And ate. Finally, I held up my clean plate for Aunt Bridey's inspection. She looked unimpressed. I scowled, thinking that I could pull a rabbit out of the empty teapot and Aunt Bridey would still look unimpressed. Then I thought of something that I knew would impress her.

"You know what, Aunt Bridey? Last night, Josh was, like, dazzlingly brave. The way he came flying out of that dumbwaiter and slammed into Biggs like a freight train? He was amazing. He was *fierce*."

Aunt Bridey sniffed.

"Naturally, he was. That boy's got more courage in his pinkie finger than most people have in their entire bodies. Now tell me something I don't know."

It was clear that thinking of something Aunt Bridey didn't already know would take hours, possibly even years. I said, "How about if I just get dressed instead?"

She smiled. "Now, that's the first good idea you've had all morning."

CHAPTER FOURTEEN

Josh
1938

I WAS A LITTLE NERVOUS, WAITING for Margaret
O'Malley in the abandoned shed down the street from the
infirmary among the paint rollers and mop buckets and
rusty barbed wire. Not because I was afraid she'd stand
me up. I knew she'd come. She was Margaret O'Malley. I
just didn't know what kind of shape she'd be in when she
arrived. Truth be told, when I'd left her the night before,
she hadn't looked too good, and she wasn't making much
sense.

"Nice glasses," I said, when she slipped in. "You look
like—"

"I know. Aunt Bridey told me. A movie star," she
interrupted.

"—one of the three blind mice," I finished.

She grabbed an old boot from a pile beside the door

and threw it at me. This was reassuring, even though I was surprised when she missed. Maybe, I told myself, the sunglasses had thrown off her aim.

"Let's go to the infirmary," I said, "and reconnoiter."

"First, let's have a look around," she replied.

"Actually," I started to explain, "that's what 'reconnoiter' means——"

She gave me a shove and snickered. "I know what it means! Gotcha!"

The Victory infirmary wasn't anything special, just a two-story brick building near the train depot. Through the windows, you could see the front desk, a couple of chairs, and the elevator.

In the rear, there was a beat-up old service door.

"What's that for?" asked Margaret, pointing to the crate by the back steps.

"It's where the milkman leaves the milk," I said, "for Cookie."

"Who's Cookie?" she asked.

"The cook," I said. "I met him while Preston was here."

"How many people work here?" wondered Margaret.

"Not many," I replied. "Even back before the massacre, Doc O'Malley usually just went to people's houses. But there's one nurse, or two if you count the lady who snoozes at the desk, an orderly, a cleaning lady, and Cookie. Boy, that milk crate looks like a handy-dandy place to plant the explosive device."

Margaret was quiet for a few seconds. I guess she was starting to realize I'd already done a load of reconnoitering, sometimes known as looking around, without her. Maybe another girl would've been happy that her friend had gone out and done so much work ahead of time. Margaret was not that girl.

"What time did you get here this morning anyway? The crack of dawn?" she snapped, whipping off her sunglasses and narrowing her sizzling eyes at me.

"Uh, yeah, w-well," I stammered, "after Biggs came to tell Luke about his dad, I was so riled up that I couldn't sleep, and I just wanted to get on with things, you know, do some pre-reconnoitering I guess you could say, just laying the groundwork so to speak, and so I—"

"It was *before* the crack of dawn, wasn't it?" she demanded. "You left me a note telling me to meet you at ten a.m., came here in the pitch-dark, and started doing it all without me."

"Aunt Bridey said you needed your sleep after, well, everything that happened, and with the overstaying. I just wanted to make sure we had time," I protested. "After all, you're . . ."

"What? Weak? Babyish? A girl?"

"No!"

"What then?"

I just hauled off and said it: "Running out of time."

All she had to say to that was, "Oh." Like it hit her in a funny place, too.

Then she said, "Hold on, partner, *explosive* device? We're bombing the infirmary? No offense, but that sounds really stupid. And illegal. And won't Aristotle be *in* the infirmary?"

"We're not using a bomb. We're using a blasting cap," I said.

"Right," she muttered. "Oh. That's totally different. Sure. A blasting cap. Whatever that is."

"I'll filch one from the mine," I explained. "When it blows in the milk crate, it'll be our diversion. So we can get Aristotle down the elevator—supposing he's on the second floor, if that's where he is—and out the door, and onto the donkey."

"Aunt Bridey's short-legged donkey?"

"No, the rocket-powered donkey the little men from space are bringing to take Aristotle to Neptune," I said.

"Ha, ha," she laughed, and then choked, and then threw a coughing fit worthy of Preston.

"Margaret?" I said uncertainly. By now, we had reconnoitered our way back to the abandoned shed, and I whisked her inside. When she could breathe again, she was white as a ghost and I was considering checking *her* into the infirmary.

"Overstaying," she gasped, catching her breath as she sank to the floor. "Listen. If something happens—if time runs out, and I'm so weak I can't—make it there myself—get me to the white gazebo on the hillside above town. It's where I have to be—at midnight—to get back."

"Okay, Margaret," I stammered. "I will—but how will I know?"

"You'll know," she said, grimacing. And then after a pause, she said, "Hey! Hold on! Did you say Biggs came to Luke's tent to tell him about Aristotle?"

And for some reason, as we sat there amid stripes of sunlight falling through the dusty windows onto the floor around us, I punched the wall. It scared Margaret. It scared me. And it hurt.

"He lied, Margaret!" I said. "He lied about everything. Biggs told Luke the worst lies anybody could've told him. It was almost like he knew what Luke would believe, and what would do the most damage."

"He told Luke," Margaret began quietly, "that Mr. Ratliff really never planned to compromise at all. He said Mr. Ratliff was actually one hundred percent behind the detectives, and the rules, and the guns. He said Mr. Ratliff wanted to teach the miners, especially Aristotle, a lesson."

"Yeah—right—how did you know?" I asked. But I guessed the answer to my own question. "Oh—because all Biggs's lies are going to turn into what everybody believes about Aristotle, now and for all time, all the way to your time?"

Margaret shrugged sadly.

"You should have heard the way Biggs told it, though," I said. "Like he'd made up the whole story especially for Luke. And you should've seen how Luke listened. Like he'd been waiting to hear it. Biggs just waltzed right into his tent at one in the morning, while people were still running around in the streets hollering about the murder. He sat down in Aristotle's chair at their breakfast table and made Luke sit down across from him."

"Did they invite you in?" Margaret asked. "How did you hear all this?"

"Stuck my head under the tent flap and eavesdropped," I confessed. "Flap-dropped. Something."

"Good boy," said Margaret with a sad smile.

"Biggs told Luke that Aristotle's plan never had a chance of working, and didn't deserve to work anyway, because it was pathetic and weak. And Luke looked at him and said, 'You're right. I told him we had to fight.' And Biggs said, 'Smart boy.'"

"Biggs doesn't just want to beat the miners," mused Margaret softly. "He doesn't just want to ruin Aristotle. He wants to keep Aristotle's son as a trophy. Luke is the icing on his horrible cake."

"Then Biggs told Luke the rest of his lies. He said Mr.

Ratliff ordered Aristotle to head back to Canvasburg and tell the shiftless miners it was all over. Biggs said Ratliff ordered Aristotle to admit to all of Canvasburg that he'd been wrong from the start with his letters and his protesting, and to tell them it was time to go back to the mine, with a pay cut for punishment, and to be thankful for that much. Biggs told Luke his daddy turned as yellow-bellied as a sapsucker. He told Luke Aristotle demanded ten thousand dollars on the spot and a mule to ride over the mountain. He wanted to scram then and there and run away from everything, even Luke. Biggs told Luke that was when Ratliff laughed in his father's face and called him a coward. And then, Biggs said to Luke, your daddy went loony and killed Theodore Ratliff."

Margaret flinched at the sound of that.

"But the thing is, Luke *knows* his dad would never kill anybody," I said after I thought it over some more. "Even if he really *does* think Aristotle is a weakling. Even if he *has* been mad for so long because Aristotle wouldn't let him fight that it's done something to his brain. Even if he *wants* to believe his dad's way failed. Underneath it all, there's no way Luke could think Aristotle would commit murder and run out on everybody in Canvasburg. Luke loves his dad. I know he does. He *has* to."

That's when the terrible look crossed Margaret's face.

"Josh?" she said shakily.

"Yeah?"

"*You* have to love your father," she said. "*I* have to love my father. It's who we are. It's the way we're made. But what if Luke—"

I said, "No."

"I hate to say this as much as you hate to hear it, but listen," she pressed. "What if our plan works? What if we get Aristotle out, send him across those mountains into New Mexico and bring Luke to him, and Luke won't go? What if he crosses over to Biggs's side anyway?"

"No."

"Josh," she said. *"What if saving Aristotle doesn't save your friend?"*

She was one tough cookie. Not afraid to look the worst directly in the eye. "Stop," I pleaded. "It will. I know it will. *I know Luke.* Luke is good. I feel it like I feel my own bones inside me."

At this, Margaret O'Malley stared at me like I'd just hung the moon. Then she smiled and said, "That's good enough for me."

CHAPTER FIFTEEN

Margaret
1938

OUR PLAN TO SAVE ARISTOTLE was crazy, and the craziest thing about it was that, except for two unexpected bumps in the road—later, I'd think of them as Bump One and Bump Two, like something out of Dr. Seuss—the plan went just the way we'd hoped it would.

Between the effects of overstaying, which were getting worse by the minute, and Aunt Bridey's scorching green stare down with the nurse on duty, it wasn't hard to get me admitted to the infirmary, where I was one of two patients, the other being easy to find since his room was at the other end of the second-floor hallway from mine and was marked with a sign that said PRISONER.

Once I was there, the plan went like clockwork: at nightfall, when the orderly dimmed the lights so that we all could sleep (including him, it turned out, in a chair outside Aristotle's door), I sneaked downstairs, located the night nurse (she was in the kitchen, smoking cigarettes and listening to a radio soap opera), slipped past her to the back door, opened it, collected the rope that Josh had left in the milk crate, gave one mourning dove call, got an answering one from Josh, went to my room, got under the blanket, which smelled so much like bleach my eyes watered, and waited.

At least I was supposed to wait, but it had been a while since I'd had any of Aunt Bridey's tea or food—and the hospital food in 1938 made its twenty-first-century counterpart look like the food of the gods—so I was woozy and my head felt like someone was beating on it with a rubber mallet, and I dozed off. I woke up maybe half an hour later to find the light in my room burning and Bump One standing at the foot of my bed, looking for all the world like Aunt Bridey with a mustache.

I sat up and snatched my movie star sunglasses as fast as I could, but as I fumbled to slip them on, the mustachioed Aunt Bridey said, "Don't bother. I've already seen them."

"What do you mean?" I said in my best sweet-little-girl voice, which I had to admit wasn't all that great. It didn't help that my heart was bouncing around the inside of my chest like a demented frog.

Doc O'Malley, because who else could it have been, didn't answer, just came to the side of my bed, whisked out a thermometer, shook it, and said, "Open."

I opened and sat there with the thing clamped firmly under my tongue as the doc took my pulse and shone his flashlight into first one eye, then the other.

"Foolish girl," he said, angrily, "foolish, foolish girl. Don't you know you're playing with fire?"

The first thing I thought of was the blasting caps, which Josh might have been planting in the milk crate even as I lay there, helpless. I started to speak, to tell the doc something like "Who, me? I hate explosions. I don't even like to be in the same room with matches, sweet little girl that I am," but Doc O'Malley gestured to the thermometer and gave one sharp shake of his head to shut me up.

"I hear you're staying with my sister," he said, grimly, "who is no doubt aiding and abetting in whatever desperately misguided scheme you've undertaken."

He slid out the thermometer. Whatever he read on it made him make a *tsk* sound and look madder than ever, so it took me a second to realize what he'd just said.

"Your *sister*?" But of course Aunt Bridey was his sister. "But that makes you—"

"Don't!" he barked. "Don't tell me who you are. I shouldn't even be talking to you."

He was my great-grandfather. I'd known that, of course. The information had been rattling around inside my crowded brain for some time, but it was one thing to know a fact and a totally other thing to have it standing in the same room, taking your temperature and glaring at you.

"Look at your eyes, glowing like lanterns," he said with disgust. "I saw my sister in this state often enough. You'll feel even worse after your return home, and it will serve you right."

He smacked the bedside table with his hand, making me jump.

"Good God, child! What is it? Are you just a fool? Or does no one in your time take the forswearing to heart?"

Before I could answer, he said, "No. Don't answer that. I can't know anything about who you are or where you're from. All I know is that you must go back there, now. Tonight. This second, if possible."

"But I can't!" I cried. "I have to save my . . ."

The look on his face stopped me.

"Please," I said, "I do take the forswearing to heart. I wouldn't be here if it weren't a matter of life and death."

Doc O'Malley gave a harsh laugh.

"Life and death. By traveling, you may be endangering more lives than you can comprehend. You are flying in the face of history!"

Maybe I was callous, but I couldn't think about the lives I might be endangering. There just wasn't room in my head. I could only think of my beautiful father in his bare cell facing certain death. And Aristotle doing the same thing a few doors down.

Aristotle! If anyone could help us free him, it was the doc. He was a doctor. Hadn't he taken some kind of oath to keep people alive?

I took hold of the doctor's coat sleeve and said, as fast as I could before he could stop me, "I need to free Aristotle Agrippa. Will you help me?"

The doc flew back like I'd bitten him. He clamped his hands over his ears.

"For God's sake, child, don't speak another word. Just go back to wherever you came from. I beg you. From this moment on, as soon as I exit this room, *you do not exist for me.*"

Without another glance in my direction, he switched off the light, walked out the door, and closed it soundlessly behind him.

I lay in the dark, shivering with fever and fear, cocooned inside the smelly blanket, waiting for whatever awful thing would happen next, but what happened was . . . exactly nothing. The hours dragged by, until I knew that the time for the next part of our plan must be drawing near. The overstaying had turned my fingers clumsy, but I managed to put on my shoes, pulled the heavy coil of rope out from where I'd hidden it under the bed, and clutched it to my chest, waiting, waiting.

Then—*BOOM BOOM BOOM!* The noise was thunderous, way louder and longer lasting than I'd expected. Josh said there'd be a small explosion, enough to get people running to discover the cause, but to me, it sounded like he'd just blown the back door off the place and the milk crate to smithereens.

Fueled by a burst of adrenaline, I slipped out into the hallway in time to see the orderly disappear at a run down the stairs; then I threw the rope in the wheelchair and tugged it—a big, brown, unwieldy wicker number— out of my room, ran with it down the hallway, and burst through Aristotle's door.

He lay handcuffed to the bed, conscious but groggy, confused, and only slightly more lively than when I'd seen him last, bleeding on the parquet floor of the cigar parlor.

"Hello, Mr. Agrippa." I said, "it's an honor to meet you."

"Who are you?" he asked, weakly, his hand pressed to the bandage on his head.

"We're saving you," I told him.

I had the urge to hug him, but there wasn't time. There wasn't a moment to lose. I whirled around, looking for a place to tie the rope, and found that, as Aunt Bridey had predicted, Aristotle's metal bed was bolted to the floor. I tied the rope to one of its posts, using the knot Aunt Bridey had shown me. Then I unlatched and pushed open the casement window, and mourning doved at the top of my lungs.

For a terrible second, nothing happened, and then there was Josh, Aunt Bridey's bolt cutters strapped to his back. He didn't waste time waving up at me, just seized the bottom of the rope and started to climb. I held my breath, since this was the most uncertain part of the plan, relying as it did on the strength of one extremely scrawny, spaghetti-armed kid. Maybe it was adrenaline again, maybe it was because Josh had been a jewel thief or a spider in another life, but whatever it took to scramble up that wall, Josh must've had it, because in a surprisingly short time I was helping him over the sill and he was *in*!

I could hear voices outside the building and smell smoke, and I figured that we still had some time to work with, although not much. But we were almost there! All we needed to do was cut Aristotle's handcuffs, help him into the wheelchair, and get him down the elevator, out the front door, and into the woods where the donkey waited to carry him to Aunt Bridey's and then, as soon as possible, over the mountains to New Mexico, where we would reunite him with his son.

And that's when we hit Bump Two.

Aristotle wouldn't go.

As Josh began to wrangle with the bolt cutters, and I feverishly whispered a nutshell version of our plan into

Aristotle's one bandage-free ear, he reached over and took Josh gently by the wrist.

"No, Josh. I cannot go. Please leave before you are caught," he said.

We stared at him.

"But you have to go!" Josh whispered. "They'll kill you if you stay."

"I don't think so," said Aristotle.

"No!" I said. "They will. We know they will!"

"The miners must not believe I would run. They will lose heart, and that must not happen. They must know I stood by them. Please, you go!"

Before I knew it was happening, I was crying. I grabbed Aristotle's hand.

"Please, please, please come! You don't know how much depends upon it."

That's when we heard the footsteps on the stairs.

"You'll die!" cried Josh.

I've never seen anything as at peace as Aristotle's face when he said, "Better to die than to run. Now, go."

We went. What else was there to do? If we were caught, I might die in 1938. Josh might be sent to prison himself. At least if we were free, there was still a chance. Josh went first so that he could help me when I got to the end of the rope. My body throbbed, my head seethed with what felt like lava, and a few yards from the bottom, my arms just gave out. Josh didn't so much catch me as break my fall, but he got up and was helping me half crawl, half stagger into the trees when I remembered the rope still tied to the bed. They'd probably already found it! And then they would come after us for sure.

"The rope!" I whispered. "It'll give us away!"

"Oh no! Maybe I can go back for it."

Josh and I spun wildly around—and froze.

The rope wasn't dangling from the window anymore. Instead, someone was standing there, holding it bundled in his arms. I could see the man's face clear as day because he was looking right at me. Doc O'Malley. Without a word, he dropped the bundle. It landed with a soft thud on the grass, and Josh ran and picked it up. I never took my eyes off the doc, my great-grandfather, taking care of me despite his better judgment. He made a sweeping gesture with his arm, one that meant, "Go!" Then he pulled the window shut and vanished into the room.

CHAPTER SIXTEEN

Josh
1938

"THAT CAN'T BE ALL," MARGARET insisted, gazing desperately at the night sky above us, but the sky wasn't listening. She turned her eyes to me. I don't know how much it hurt her to stay as long as she had, but I know history took a dim view of every single move she was making, growing more and more indignant. She was supposed to be long gone—of course, she wasn't supposed to have come at all—and every second she stayed was a battle. She slowly sank to the ground, hidden with me in the brush in the vacant lot across from the infirmary, and she dropped her head between her knees, her fists clenched. "There must be something else. Something we haven't thought of."

The clock in city hall gave us eight minutes until midnight. Margaret was already so beat, she had a fever of, I don't know, about a hundred and nineteen. I had no idea how it'd gotten so late. My mind had been nothing but confetti in a whirlwind since we'd sneaked out of Aristotle's room. "You have to get to the gazebo," I said. "All we can do now is get you home."

"Aristotle," she pleaded.

Seven minutes.

"Aristotle."

The first time I'd ever laid eyes on him, he'd been doing something kind—kicking my dad's yellow helmet down C Street in the dark to make him laugh, to ease his fear of the mine, to make friends. All Aristotle Agrippa had ever done, his whole life, was help. All those letters, all those nights climbing back and forth over the mountain to keep Canvasburg alive. He'd stood up in front of bullets. He'd gotten Preston a trumpet. He'd done everything a human being could do for his friends. He'd sat in a room with one of the most powerful men in the world and convinced him to do what was right. Aristotle had nearly seen his dream come true. And now he lay, broken and weak, in an infirmary bed with no one to stand up for him, while, somewhere nearby, death made its way toward him.

"We c-could stay," I stammered. "I could watch the door . . ." I knew it was ridiculous. The people who came for Aristotle would be killers, hard and cold, as bad or worse than the men who'd shot at us from the safety of their tank. I'd be about as much of a nuisance to them as a swarm of fruit flies. But—if I could slow them down. Make noise. Kick up a fuss. Set a trap—a blasting cap— use the rope for a trip wire—yeah—

Five minutes to midnight. Margaret slumped against me, and only at the last second did I gather my wits enough to catch her before she slid to the ground. She was barely breathing. She'd overstayed, badly. She wouldn't last another day. If I didn't get her to the mountainside by midnight, if she wasn't awake enough to do whatever she needed to do or see whatever she needed to see, she'd end up trapped for eternity in some forgotten eddy of time. Or maybe she wouldn't even be able to begin her journey. Maybe she'd end up stuck with me in 1938 and die here before another midnight. But maybe I could get her to the mountainside, and safely on her way, and make it back down to the front door of the infirmary before the thugs came for Aristotle.

I picked up Margaret like a sack of feed and took off running for the white gazebo.

As I turned the first corner, I nearly came face-to-face with them. Three men like bulls, breathing hard in the night air, stamping and shifting their feet as they got ready to do what they were going to do. Luckily, they were so intent on the crime they were about to commit, they didn't see Margaret and me, and I managed to duck into an alleyway as the leader punched one of his buddies in the arm and spat on the ground.

The sight of them brought Margaret to life again. It was like she was a hundred-pound house cat and my task was to drop her in a bathtub. A wild strength radiated from inside her, desperation, something that felt not very different from what I'd felt in Elijah Biggs.

"No!" cried Margaret, shoving me, pummeling me, scratching at my face. "Stop them! Get Aristotle—I'll take him away with me where they can't find him—I can't—I can't—I can't—"

I clamped my hand over her mouth and hoped to high heaven the murderers hadn't heard. But they hadn't. Maybe history didn't want them to. They crunched down the gravel street toward the infirmary.

I had to decide. Save Aristotle or save Margaret. Not that I was sure I'd be able to do either one.

I chose Margaret O'Malley.

She wilted in my arms as the footsteps died away in the street. And I ran faster than I had ever run in my life. Uphill. In the dark.

I got her there. With seconds to spare. I helped her sit, and shook her awake, because I knew she had to be conscious for this to work, awake enough to see her way back home. "I'm going to miss you, Margaret," I told her. "I've never had a friend like you."

"I've never had a friend like you, either," whispered Margaret.

She began slipping into some sort of trance, but she fought her way out of it to tell me something else: "Take care of Luke. Whatever happens. Do your best. Don't give up on him."

"I won't," I said.

"Ever," she said.

"Ever," I replied.

"Promise," she said.

"I promise," I promised.

"And don't forget, I'll see you again one day," Margaret reminded me.

"I can't wait," I said.

"Good-bye."

"Good-bye."

She unclenched her right fist, and in her palm lay a piece of cloth and black fountain pen, Aristotle's belongings from the hunting lodge floor.

"I can't carry anything with me," she whispered.

I took them from her and shoved them into my pocket. Then Margaret looked up at the stars, and I did, too, and when I looked back, she was gone.

CHAPTER SEVENTEEN

Margaret
2014

THIS TIME, THE TRIP WAS WORSE. The peaceful part was just a few heartbeats long, and when the pain came, hammering me from every side, including and especially from the inside, I didn't have the heart to fight it. For the first time in all my thirteen years, I honestly did not give a flying plate of squirrel scat what happened to me. I gave up, gave in. I was like the sea lion I'd seen once on a nature show, and time was a pod of orcas tossing me around like a toy, flinging me into the air in a game of torture hacky sack until time decided to chomp me, once and for all, in its big, mean, grinning jaws.

But the chomp never came. Instead, I was thrown, with a bone-shuddering thud, flat onto my back, into the kind of ordinary quiet that is really made up of small night sounds and, even before I could muster enough energy to wrench open my eyes, I knew I was home. It *smelled* like 2014, although until that moment, I hadn't known that 2014 had a smell. And if I was smelling it, then that meant I was *breathing*, which dead people never do, a fact that should've made me happy, but I was beyond caring, beyond hope. Alive, maybe, but alive like a moth is alive after someone's ripped off its wings.

But remember "equilibrium"? My favorite word? My little habit of searching for any ragtag piece of good to balance out the bad? What I found out right then is that sometimes you don't find equilibrium. It finds you. Sometimes the good you need puts its hands on your shoulders in the nick of time and says your name, twice— "Margaret! Margaret!"—and not just in any old voice, but a voice you know, one you can't remember ever not knowing. Charlie's voice.

And this wasn't just some ragtag piece of good; this was good with all its flags flying and its trumpets blowing, because I opened my eyes and saw his face, looking just exactly the way it always had, and that's when it hit me, clear as starlight through my fog of pain, that there is a flip side, a blessed side to history resisting. Maybe the bad things you wanted to change were still there, but so were the good things, the things you loved best and wouldn't want changed for anything in the world.

"You're here," I croaked.

Charlie gave a sheepish grin and said, "Yeah, I know

you told me to leave, but I couldn't do it. So I sat over there under a tree, just kind of keeping watch. But you're right; it took almost no time at all. None of our time, I mean."

"No," I said, "you're *here*. You're you."

I reached up and touched his hair, still weirdly tidy from when he'd cut it for the trial.

"You even have the same stupid haircut."

I hadn't disappeared Charlie. I hadn't tripped off some chain of events that caused him not to be or to be somebody else. The thought that I could have was like an icy hand at my throat—how had I not even thought of that before? *Because you couldn't let yourself*, I thought, *because if you had, you wouldn't have been able to go try to save your dad.*

"For your information, a lot of people like this haircut," he said, with his same old usual voice.

And for that tiny space of time, there was no room for Aristotle or failure or grief. There was only room for: thank you, thank you, thank you, thank you.

Then Charlie's face blurred and doubled before my eyes, and I thought for a second I was passing out or dying or getting pulled back through time again. But I was only crying, tears of sweet relief to cool my burning cheeks.

My mother thought I had the flu, and I thought it best not to tell her that actually I was suffering from acute overstaying complicated by a brutal bout of time travel compounded by my total failure to save Aristotle Agrippa or Luke Agrippa or my father or anyone or anything at all.

After my sudden and glorious realization that Charlie was Charlie, the rest of that night is hazy. But somehow, I ended up on my living room sofa, still in my mothball sweater but out of my giant shoes, covered with the Hudson Bay blanket from the cedar chest, and sweating like a rain forest. My mom found me there the next morning and carried me to my room, where I began my recovery, although things got a lot worse before they got better.

For days, my whole body throbbed with something like a migraine, including my bones and my internal organs. I'm not sure where my spleen is, but I'm pretty sure it was throbbing. The worst part, though, was the places my poor mind wandered to when I slept. Dark places, places so grim, empty, and sad that I'd wake up crying and calling for my mother every time.

The good news is that my mother came, every time. She brought me tea and sat in the armchair next to my bed with her tiny book light, and softly read and read, for hours, all my favorite books, and even when I was too exhausted to really listen, just the sound of my mom's voice was enough. Even when my skin hurt so that I couldn't stand to be touched, my mother's voice, all the familiar ups and downs of it, wrapped all the way around me and *held*.

Then one day, I woke up hungry as a stray cat, starving for sunlight and food, in that order, so I threw off my covers and jumped out of bed. Since I basically hadn't eaten for six days, I got instantly light-headed and had to sit down and put my head between my knees until the paparazzi flashbulbs stopped going off in front of my eyes. But somehow I not only made it to the window and opened the shade but also managed to drag the armchair across the room, so that I could curl up on it and let the tangerine-colored light wash over me.

That's where my mom found me. Anyone who comes into a room with a plate of brioche and sliced peaches would look good to a person as hungry as I was, but I swear my mother was glowing.

"Look at you!" she said, smiling. "I knew you'd feel better today."

"How'd you know?" I asked, taking a shark-sized bite of the brioche.

"I came in and sat with you for a while last night. You were sleeping so peacefully, none of that tossing and turning."

"Have I been tossing and turning?"

"Like a fish out of water, flop, flop, flop. And then there was the groaning. And the teeth grinding."

"Nice," I said. I bared my teeth at her. "They still seem to work."

"So I see," she said, eyeing the crumbs on my plate. "Let me get you some more food, and then I have some news."

By the way her eyes were sparkling, I knew it was good news. I thought fleetingly about telling her to forget the food and just tell me, but my stomach was calling the shots. When I had inhaled another warm brioche and had my hands firmly wrapped around a mug of lemony tea, my mother told me the news. She'd gotten a call the morning after I'd fallen ill from a professor at a law school in Tempe. He was part of a group of lawyers and law students who worked to free the wrongly convicted.

"They're a national organization called Team Exoneration. Their success rate is amazing," said my mom. "And they want to work on your dad's case! They think there's a good chance they can get him released!"

I felt dazzled, like she'd just handed me the moon. For almost a minute, I couldn't even speak.

Finally, I squeaked, "When?"

"They met with Roland Wise three days ago! They've already started!"

"So he could be out soon! Like before the summer! We can have a party and invite everyone and maybe go to the beach like we always talk about! Maybe Charlie and his family can all come, too, and maybe . . ."

That's when I noticed that a cloud, just a little one, was scudding across the sunny landscape of my mother's face.

"Or maybe we can just keep him to ourselves," I amended. "Just stay home and cook out and go on desert walks and be normal? That would be nice, right?"

But the cloud didn't scud away. It just stayed, casting its small shadow into my mom's blue eyes.

"Maybe soon," she said, gently, "but probably not that soon. I read about some of the other Team Exoneration cases. It can take a bit of time."

"Oh," I said. "Like months?"

"Sometimes. Sometimes longer, even years. But not always."

I almost said "oh" again. No, the truth is, I almost said, "Oh, no, not *years*!" But I caught myself in the nick of time. When your mother has come into your room with a big shining gift of hope and a smile like you haven't seen on her face in what feels like ten centuries, you don't wreck it.

So instead, I smiled and said, "What matters is that they believe in him, and they're good at what they do, and we'll get him home with us in the end."

My mother leaned over, smoothed back my hair, which was a pile of knots and none too clean, and kissed me on the forehead.

"Yes," she said, softly, "and meanwhile, we've got each other, right?"

It hit me right then how, even though we both were desperate for my dad to come home, "each other" was a lot to have; "each other" just might see us through.

"Heck yeah, we have each other," I said. "The unstoppable O'Malley women, together forever!"

My mother rested her hand on my very dirty hair, again, with one of those full, endlessly tender looks mothers give that can make you cry if you're not careful.

"I'm proud of you," she said.

"I'm proud of you, too," I said. "Can I take a shower now?"

Her laugh was like money falling from the sky. "Heck, yeah!" she said.

Charlie stopped by that afternoon. Actually, according to my mom, he'd stopped by every afternoon since I'd gotten back from 1938 (my mother didn't say that exactly, of course), but this time, she told him to go on up and see me. I heard him running up the stairs, clomping like an elephant with his big feet, but when he got to the door of my room, he stopped and stood there with this look on his face that was part shy, part wary, like I was an endangered species, fragile but possibly also about to bite him.

"Hey," he said.

"Hey," I said, "you coming in or what?"

"Sure," he said, but all he did was sort of sidle past the doorjamb and lean against the wall.

"What?"

"What?"

"Why are you acting so sketchy?" I said. I threw my stuffed owl at him. It hit him in the chest.

Charlie shrugged and scratched his head.

"Well, gee, Margaret, I don't know. It's not like you just traveled through time and back or anything. It's not like the last time I saw you, you looked ninety-nine percent dead. It's not like you've been insanely sick for an entire week, and I wasn't sure if you would make it. Why would I feel awkward in this situation? That's just so silly of me."

"Shut up," I said, laughing.

He walked over and plopped down in the armchair.

"Thanks for carrying me home," I said.

"Well, it was either that or leave you there for the coyotes to eat."

I took a breath. "I didn't save him."

I realized right after I said it that "him" could mean one of a number of people, and I thought about clarifying things for Charlie, but then I realized that it didn't matter. I hadn't saved any of them.

"Well, I figured, since your dad is still in prison."

I don't know why I hadn't thought of that. Of course, Charlie already knew I hadn't saved anyone, since the whole point of saving Luke would've been to keep my dad out of prison, and he was still there.

"But you tried," said Charlie. "You did your best, probably risked your life over and over without even giving it a second thought, knowing you."

His cheeks went red when he said this.

"That doesn't matter," I said. "I failed."

"Hey, it *does* matter," said Charlie, sitting up straight in the armchair. "It matters to Grandpa Joshua. It would matter to a lot more people, if they knew. And it matters to me."

His cheeks went redder.

"Thanks," I said, and meant it with all my heart, even though I knew better than to mention the heart part.

"So," I said, "I guess you want to hear what happened? You've been in limbo for, like, a week, which had to be tough."

Charlie looked startled at this.

"Well, yeah. Sure. I mean, I heard some of it from Grandpa Joshua, but I definitely want to hear it from your perspective."

And there was something else I hadn't thought of. Here I'd been thinking Charlie had been on pins and needles all this time, waiting to hear my story, when he'd already heard it because it wasn't just mine. It was Grandpa Joshua's, too. It hadn't been before I'd traveled, but now it was. Because Grandpa Joshua, Charlie's grandfather, was also my coconspirator, my friend Josh.

"Oh. Right," I said, shaking my head. "You know what?

For someone who actually time traveled, I'm having a lot of trouble getting my mind around the whole idea."

Charlie grinned. "Well, yeah, it only forces you to rethink everything you ever learned about the way the world works and the laws of physics, not to mention logic and common sense. Anyway, I hear Picasso and Harriet Tubman had trouble with it, too, so don't feel bad."

"You want to hear my story now? Because I had been feeling like I wanted to put it behind me forever, but suddenly, I realize that if I don't talk about it to someone, I might explode."

"That would be messy," said Charlie. "So you'd better go ahead and tell."

I did. I told and told, every sad, terrible, funny, beautiful (it wasn't until I was telling it that I realized there actually *were* beautiful parts), scary, heart-wrenching bit of it, paying special attention to the moments when Josh had been a hero, since I knew he'd downplayed those to Charlie. Afterward, I felt drained, but not in a bad way, and also sort of awestruck by all that had happened. Even if it hadn't happened in my lifetime, it had happened in my *life*, and I would carry it with me forever.

"But in the end, Charlie, I failed. I let everyone down."

"Shut up," Charlie said. "You were amazing. You and Grandpa Joshua, both."

Suddenly, I remembered those last moments: me limp

as a sack of potatoes in Josh's arms; the men rushing in to murder Aristotle; above us all, removed from life and death, hope and love, the ruthlessly glittering stars; and Josh, oh Josh, turning away from the infirmary toward The Octagon, away from saving Aristotle, toward saving me.

"It isn't fair," I murmured.

"What?" asked Charlie.

"It was my father, my quest. But in the end, Josh had to do the hardest part of all. It must have been terrible, that moment when he had to choose."

Charlie nodded. "But he chose right. You're here. If you weren't here, if you'd never come back—"

He broke off, and we sat in silence, not looking at each other. Then Charlie brightened.

"Hey, your mom told me about Team Exoneration! That's awesome!"

I smiled. "Yep! It could take a while for them to get him out, but that's okay. As long as we all have that to look forward to, we can wait. We've got time."

As it turned out, I was wrong. Time was exactly what we didn't have.

Two days later, I came home from school to find my mom gone and our neighbor Mrs. Darley waiting for me. I hadn't even gotten my key into the front door lock when she opened the door and said, "Before I say anything else, I want you to know that he's going to be okay. Dr. AJ drove your mom to the hospital, and she spoke to his surgeon personally, right before they wheeled him in, and she swore up and down that your dad's going to make it."

The world seemed to go wavy under me, and I almost had to sit down right on the porch, but Mrs. Darley caught me under the arms. She started to pull me into a hug, but I held out my hand to stop her.

"Just tell me," I whispered, "please."

Tears filled her kind brown eyes. "He was stabbed in the prison yard. Oh, honey, someone tried to kill your father."

Dr. AJ was right, as always. My dad was going to be okay. We got the news later that night that the surgery was successful, and he was out of the woods. But what everyone knew, even before Roland Wise said it out loud, was that he wasn't going to stay out of the woods. Once he recovered, my father had to return to prison, where at least one person wanted to make very sure that he went back into those woods, this time for good.

"Our best hope is to get him protective custody," said Mr. Wise.

He had met my mother in the hospital the night before and then come over to our house the next day.

"What's that?" asked my mother. "Solitary confinement? John would hate that."

"I know," said Mr. Wise, "but it would just be until they caught the person who did this."

At this, my mother gave him a calm, level, unwavering, slate-blue stare.

"Do you think they will?" she asked.

Mr. Wise hesitated and sighed. "I doubt it. A yard full of witnesses and no one's talking. Somebody spray-painted the lens of the nearest surveillance camera orange, and the weapon's vanished into thin air. I'm not saying it's impossible, but even if they catch the individual who did it, well, someone else might try again."

"It's because of Team Exoneration, isn't it?" asked my mother bitterly. "Victory Corp. wants to make that investigation go away."

I jerked my head up to look at Mr. Wise. Team Exoneration couldn't be putting my father in danger! Team Exoneration was going to save him.

"Well, if that investigation continues, it could turn up some extremely ugly skeletons in the Victory Corporation's closet. It would be in the company's interests to silence John as a witness in his own defense and to send Team

Exoneration packing."

My mother's hands were shaking so hard, she had to press them together to make them stop.

"Roland, we need to find a way to get John out of there. You know and I know that even if protections are put in place, they'll find a way to get to him."

"I hear you. I do. Unfortunately, the police here consider John's case closed. I'm working on an appeal, but Team Exoneration has resources I just don't have. They're our best bet."

Yes, I thought, *yes! Team Exoneration will handle everything!*

My mother covered her face with her long, lovely hands. Dr. AJ put an arm around each of us, and I let myself fall against her, fold into her, wanting her to take care of me, to make it all better. *I'm tired,* I thought, *I'm a kid. Let the adults handle it. Let Team Exoneration save my dad.*

I was so close to giving in, turning it all over to someone else. But then I remembered Josh, how he had saved me, and I was filled with shame. If Josh could rise up and be strong at the worst possible moment, so could I. I pulled out from under Dr. AJ's arm, opened my eyes, and asked the question I had to ask.

"What if Team Exoneration went away? What if we told them to go, give up the case? Would my father be safer in prison then?"

It was like everyone in the room froze, waiting for his answer, for Roland Wise to say for us what we all already knew.

"This is all just theoretical," he said, "but yes. I think John would be safer."

My mother's eyes locked with mine. After a second, both of us nodded.

"Get him solitary confinement, Roland," said my mother, wearily. "Keep working on the appeal. But call off Team Exoneration."

"But the Team is our best hope of proving him innocent!"

"Then we'll just have to find a better hope someplace else," I said.

I was allowed to visit him later that day. Dr. AJ took me so that my mother could get some sleep. For a second there, when I saw the police officer in a chair outside my father's hospital room door, the memory of Aristotle in the infirmary stopped me dead in my tracks. But this wasn't then, I reminded myself, and my father wasn't Aristotle; my father wasn't history; he was the living, breathing, precious now, my now.

* * *

Dr. AJ let me go in alone, but when I walked into the room, I saw another police officer sitting in a chair at the opposite end of the room from my father's bed. Because my dad appeared to be asleep, I turned to the officer, who stood up when he saw me and removed his hat. His hair was steel-gray and bristly, but his eyes were nice, velvet black and fringed with long lashes.

"Excuse me, officer," I said, "I'm Margaret O'Malley, and I was wondering if I might be able to have a few minutes alone to talk to my dad. Would that be okay? Please?"

"I'm pleased to meet you, Miss O'Malley," he said. "Name's Officer Bob Georgopoulos. Wish I could accommodate your request. I'm sure I'd feel the same in your situation, but my orders are to stay. Tell you what, though, I'll just sit over here with my book and you can forget I'm even here. Just go on and have your conversation, okay?"

He sat down and opened his book.

"Thanks," I said.

My dad's eyes were shut and his face looked oddly bare without his glasses, his eyebrows sort of floating and out of place without the thick frames to anchor them. He was paler than usual, although even pale, my ruddy dad was still sort of pink-cheeked, and he was hooked up to some tubes and machines the way people in hospital beds usually are. But he looked alive, just as alive as ever.

I touched his hand, which was warm, and he opened his eyes, which were their usual beach-glass green.

"Hey, there, sweetheart," he said. His voice was a little strange, raspy, but his smile was just exactly right.

"Hey, there, Daddy," I said.

"I'm glad to see you looking so chipper," he said. "I was worried."

"*You* were worried? You're the one who got hurt, remember?"

"I heard you'd been sick."

Suddenly, I couldn't meet his eyes. I looked down at his hand holding mine and shrugged.

"Fever, pain all over, bad headaches, weakness. And glassy eyes, bright, bright, green glassy eyes, traffic-light, go-light eyes. I've never seen anyone be sick precisely like that, but I've heard about it."

I shrugged again. He tipped my chin up so that I had to look at him. At the kindness in his face, my eyes filled with tears.

"I'm sorry," I said. "I'm so sorry."

"For breaking the forswearing?" he asked.

I weighed my answer carefully and decided that a lie at this moment would be the worst thing I could give my father.

"No," I said, "I had to try. What I'm sorry for is that I failed. I didn't change anything."

"I should scold you, you know," said my dad, "but I think I need two fully functioning kidneys in order to do it properly, so it might be a while."

I smiled through my tears at this. And then my head was on his chest. In my ear, his heartbeat was a steady thrum that felt as big and permanent and elemental as the dance of stars, the force of history. My father smoothed my hair. I could have stayed like that forever, but I had something to say and I wanted to stare straight into my dad's eyes while I did it, green to green.

"Listen," I said, "I'm going to save you, anyway. In the here and now."

"Good," said my dad.

I blinked.

"Hold on," I said. "You really believe I can?"

"Sure," my dad said, like he was surprised by my question. "You're you, for starters, and the best place to save anyone is always the here and now. Plus, most saving happens by changing human hearts and minds, and when human hearts and minds are involved, there's plenty of reason to believe."

For a second, time folded up inside my head and there was Josh in that old dusty shed, saying, "*I know Luke!*"

"Margaret?"

My dad tugged a piece of my hair to bring me back.

"Sorry, but what you said, you reminded me so much

of Grandpa Joshua. The way you keep faith in people, even though so many awful things have happened to you."

"That's because Grandpa Joshua and I bother to do the math."

"What math?"

"For every big, bad, attention-getting thing that happens, there are thousands of small good ones, acts that might even seem ordinary but really aren't, so many that we can forget to notice them or to count them up. But it's what has always amazed me: not how terrible people can be to each other, but how good, in spite of everything."

I needed time to ponder this, but already, Officer Georgopoulos was getting up, clearing his throat, saying it was time for me to go. I leaned over and kissed my dad's cheek.

"I'll see you soon," I said.

"I know you will," said my dad.

All the way home in the car I was silent, but my mind was whirring and blinking like those machines back in the hospital room, so I was almost surprised Dr. AJ couldn't hear it. The way my dad said things, well, it was hard not to just accept them, but what he'd said about hearts and minds, about all the small goodnesses adding up to amazing, I needed to work that out for myself. I wanted to believe it, but there was so much awfulness looming so large all around me: my dad stabbed, Judge Biggs's voice sentencing him to death, Mr. Ratliff stabbed, Aristotle lynched, and, looming largest of all, so big he blocked the light, Elijah Biggs. Maybe I couldn't do it, have faith like Grandpa Joshua and my dad. Maybe I was too mad inside to do the math.

But then we drove down our street and it was lined with cars, and when we got to the driveway, I saw that every window in our house was a rectangle of light, and I could hear the voices even before we were out of the car.

The house was full of friends. Friends and food, casseroles and pies on every surface. Charlie's whole family, including Grandpa Joshua, the Darleys, the Blakes, the Tiklas sisters who were almost a hundred years old, a couple of my teachers, Reverend Mike from church, and there was my mother, who should've been asleep, pouring coffee into Mrs. Darley's cup, and her smile and the graceful curve her body made when she leaned to pour didn't look tired at all. And then, in my head, there were others: Aunt Bridey holding me while I shook, Officer Georgopoulos with his head stuck in his book, Doc O'Malley tossing out the rope, Josh carrying me to The Octagon while the stars pressed down.

We were all there, together, holding each other up.

And there was Charlie, coming out of the kitchen with

a stack of plates, seeing me, and putting the plates down to come talk.

"We have to save him ourselves," I told him. "You, me, and Grandpa Josh. In the here and now."

"Let's do it," said Charlie.

That night, I wrote a letter to my town, one I'd send off to our local newspaper, the *Victory Voice*. I guess I hoped they'd publish it, but that didn't matter so much to me. What mattered is that I wrote it and meant every word. It could've been a sad letter or an angry one. It could've been a rant or a moan or an ice-cold slap in the face. But I didn't want to be Luke, who let the bad turn him ugly inside. So I did the math, and I wrote a thank-you note to Victory. It took a long time.

CHAPTER EIGHTEEN

Charlie
2014

THE NEXT DAY, I FILLED MARGARET IN on some Major Vital Facts about the Great Nation of AstraZeneca.

"Location," I said, because it sounded like a very snowy place, "forty miles northwest of Greenland." You probably know this already, but Greenland is even snowier than Iceland, which, to be honest, is kind of green.

"Uh-huh," replied Margaret. She was a thousand miles away, thinking about all the things she needed to think about. But in my opinion, sometimes you just have to relax and let your mind turn to . . . AstraZeneca.

"National Pastime," I continued, "Narwhal Rasslin'."

"Yep," said Margaret absently.

"National Costume," I persisted, "the Bearskin Jumpsuit."

"The. Bear. Skin . . . ," murmured Margaret.

I know this may sound silly, but I was trying my best to take Margaret's mind off her troubles, if only for a few minutes, so I was a little peeved at the lack of attention she was devoting to my Major Vital Facts. "You're not listening!" I complained.

"I am too!" retorted Margaret.

"National Dish," I said.

"Yes?" said Margaret.

"Beef with Snow Pants."

"Mmmm," Margaret replied. "Good."

"See!" I said.

"I am listening!" she fired back. "You said Beets with—"

We stopped in front of my house. Kind of small. Sky blue, squat, and dusty. But better than a tent like my grandpa lived in when he was my age. There was a kayak in the basement my dad and I were nearly halfway finished building, and had been for three years—and the night before an algebra test, seats at my kitchen-table study sessions were harder to come by than tickets to the University of Arizona homecoming game.

Margaret must've had a bazillion things to take care of at home, but Grandpa Joshua had specifically instructed me to bring her to the guest room, where, since he'd been visiting for over a week, he now had enough laundry scattered around to outfit a polar expedition.

"Margaret . . . ," began Grandpa Joshua when he saw her.

And I guess he could've said just about anything at that moment, since he hadn't seen her for a week, or maybe seventy-six years, depending on how you were keeping score. But out of all the possibilities, what he picked was "Good girl!"

I wish I knew how he did that. I hope I learn sometime. One day I want to be able to say it all, the total totality of what needs to be said, in two words or less.

Then he hugged her. That, too. I wanted to learn how to do that.

And when she burst into tears he pressed her head against his sweater. Add that to the list.

"It didn't work! It didn't work, it didn't work, it didn't work!" Margaret sobbed. "I was sure we could save them. We had so many chances. Every time we had an idea, I thought they'd finally be safe. It's not fair!"

"I know, honey," said Grandpa Joshua. "I know."

And as she cried it out against Grandpa Joshua's sweater, I understood how much it all added up to, everything she'd seen and endured in the present *and* in the past, and I thought about how brave Margaret O'Malley really was, and all I could do was hope that, when the time came, I'd measure up.

"Thank you, Grandpa Joshua," Margaret said when she could talk again. "Thank you for choosing me that night. Even though I almost wish you—"

"It's the rightest decision I've ever made," declared Grandpa Joshua.

"There was nothing you could do to save Luke?" Margaret asked gently. "After it was over?"

"The next day," replied Grandpa Joshua, "I found him alone in his tent. I talked, but I couldn't make him hear. He'd seen his father hanging from that rafter by then. I told him it wasn't what he thought. I told him that men hired by the Victory Corporation had done it, that his father would never have taken the coward's way out and abandoned him, but he didn't hear. All he said was, 'Some people there's just no saving.'"

"Biggs had already started filling his head with lies," Margaret supplied.

"And as always, they were exactly the right lies," added Grandpa Joshua. "The poor kid couldn't help but believe them. When Biggs got him to think his dad had killed himself to escape facing the consequences of his actions, it confirmed his worst fears about his father being a coward. And when Luke was most shaken up, angry, and confused, Biggs offered to put him up in his mansion on the brick side of town.

"By then, the miners were completely beat. Anybody who hadn't slunk away into the desert had gone back into the mine. That was the beginning of a long, hard time for my family. Without so much as a peep, my father took a pay cut, worked longer hours, paid higher rent, and put up with any other punishment Biggs could think of for the rest of his life, just so we'd have a place to live. Dad was broken by what happened to his friend. Hollowed out. Bereft.

"Mom begged Luke to come live with us. I did too. But Luke was mixed up by Biggs's lies, and his confusion turned to disgust: disgust for Canvasburg, for miners, for my family, for me—for anybody in a position of weakness. Soon, there was nothing left of Luke but the smile . . ."

Grandpa Joshua's voice faded away.

"What *about* his smile, Grandpa Joshua?" pressed Margaret.

"He still . . . well . . . smiled," Grandpa Joshua faltered. Everything he'd told us so far had been hard, I knew. But what he had to say next seemed like more than he could face. "And I guess if you hadn't known him before, you'd never have been able to tell the difference. But I could tell. Preston could tell. My mom and dad could tell. Preston said it was like Luke smiled at himself . . . for smiling. Like there was some joke hidden in the middle of everything, and the joke was—nothing was the least bit funny."

Silence fell. Hard.

"That was when he got hateful?" I finally asked.

"Exactly, Charlie," said Grandpa Joshua sadly. "That was when he got hateful." And it seemed to do Grandpa Joshua a little good to put it like this, even though it was a horrible thing to have to say. I sure hope it helped.

"And now, saving him," sighed Margaret, "feels like trying to move Mount Hosta."

"I've been thinking about that," mused Grandpa Joshua. "How hard it really is to alter history."

"Me too," said Margaret.

Of course, I hadn't been through what they'd been through, so I *didn't* know how it felt, but I had enough sense to keep my mouth shut and listen, hoping to figure it out.

"And I got to wondering if," Grandpa went on, watching her closely, "maybe, just maybe, it might be possible to change history without—"

"—without changing the past!" replied Margaret excitedly. "I thought the same thing!"

And they were off to the races, speaking plain English that I couldn't understand. Change history without changing the past? What kind of sense did that make? "Grandpa?" I asked. "Can I ask one minor question? What in the heck are you guys talking about?"

"What we're talking about, Charlie," said Margaret, "is the same thing you and I talked about last night. We couldn't save Lucas in 1938. But maybe we can save him in the here and now."

"Maybe we couldn't stop Aristotle's betrayal," continued Grandpa Joshua, "and maybe we couldn't save his life, God bless him. Maybe we couldn't clear his name

219

back then and redeem his son's spirit. But maybe—maybe we can do it in the present. The old Luke Agrippa is still inside Lucas Biggs somewhere. I know it is. I know part of him still wants to believe his father was good, and strong, and to believe he himself is good and strong, too, even if he doesn't *know* that's what he wants."

I was a little bewildered by all this, but as Grandpa Joshua talked, I saw a look in his eyes that I understood. He believed in his friend. He felt the same way I'd feel if the forces of evil descended on Margaret and stole her. I'd feel awful, but I wouldn't give up on her. Grandpa Joshua had spent the last seventy years hoping for his best friend to come back, and he was *still* hoping.

"But how can we change Lucas Biggs?" asked Margaret. "We haven't got anything now we didn't have the moment he sentenced my father to death. We're as lost today as we were then. And even if we had anything new or knew anything different, why would he listen to us? Why would he believe us? What could we tell him, that I time traveled?"

"That's one thing we're never going to do." My grandfather frowned, rummaging around in the pocket of his suitcase.

"Would Judge Biggs listen to you, Grandpa Josh?" I asked.

"He hasn't for over seventy years," replied Grandpa Joshua. "I don't see why he'd start now."

"If only that old Mr. Ratliff could come back from the dead to tell him what happened in that meeting," I said. "Or if Aristotle could tell him it wasn't like he thought. No suicide. No running away. No fear. If he just could've spoken to Luke one last time. Maybe that's what Judge Biggs has been waiting for all these years. For his dad to tell him what happened."

"But the real Aristotle is gone," Margaret cried. "Without a trace. Now he's just a lie in our history book. His accomplishments, his dreams, his good name evaporated the day he died. Elijah Biggs made sure of that."

"Here," said Grandpa Joshua sadly, retrieving a battered pencil box from deep inside his suitcase. In it was nothing but a scrap of cloth and an old-fashioned fountain pen. "This is all there is of Aristotle."

"These are the things that fell out of his pocket when Elijah Biggs tried to murder him," said Margaret sadly. "I scooped them up. And when I left, I gave them to you."

"And I kept them," said Grandpa Joshua simply. "His pen and his handkerchief."

"Hold on," I said, reaching for the cloth. "Let me see that."

Margaret handed it over.

"This is a lot more than just a handkerchief," I said, looking it over.

* * *

Sometimes when I look at things long enough, they give up their secrets. Even though my brain is usually a mess and my thoughts typically swarm around like ants on a picnic blanket, when Grandpa Joshua walks with me outside of town, at night, as I stare at stars, they seem to shift until they form a message that tells me where I fit in. Not quite as spectacular as *some* people's ability to see passageways through time, but still, it comes in handy.

And as I gazed at the ragged cloth, stained brown with what we all knew was Aristotle's blood, it began to change like that. Hidden beneath the blood were shapes, shapes that formed a pattern, a design that had been very important to somebody once.

"Under the stain," I whispered. "Look. A star." And in the light of the guest bedroom, we could make out the contours of an eight-pointed star. I turned the cloth over to find the stain wasn't as heavy on the back. "It's colored," I murmured. "Gray and pink. A long time ago, it must've been black and red."

"He called it his talisman," offered Grandpa Joshua. "I thought he just meant it was his lucky handkerchief."

"Is it a quilt square?" Margaret wondered. "Or a flag?"

"It's a symbol," I declared.

"Of what?" asked Margaret.

"I don't know," I said. But now *I* was beginning to understand history, too, maybe a little like Grandpa Joshua and Margaret after all their travels and experiences. In these shapes Aristotle used to carry around in his pocket, and in the way they fit together, there was a meaning that had to do with right now.

"I couldn't bear to look at it again after you left, Margaret," lamented Grandpa Joshua. "But I couldn't bear to throw it away, either."

In one corner of the "talisman," figures appeared. Not really *appeared*. They must have been there all along, but I could suddenly see them: letters.

"'For L,'" I said, "u-k-e."

Margaret and Grandpa Joshua leaned in to look.

"I see!" yelped Margaret.

"So do I," said Grandpa Joshua, softly.

"For Luke," I said, wonderingly. "Aristotle was going to give this to Luke?"

"He had it at the meeting," said Grandpa Joshua. "This must be what they were talking about while I was trapped outside the room. The memento. Before you came in, Margaret. I heard their voices."

"This square meant something to Aristotle, something important," I continued.

"And it was supposed to mean something to Luke," added Margaret. "But Aristotle never got a chance to deliver his message."

"So we'll have to deliver it for him," I said. "After

we figure out what it means. What do we know about Aristotle? I mean, his past? Where could this have come from? What could it have meant to him? What kind of star has eight points? Do you think Aristotle has any relatives left anywhere who would know?"

"Aristotle's family stayed behind in Greece," Grandpa Joshua said slowly. "He never saw them again after he left. I think he must've made some friends in the US before he came to the coal mine in Arizona, though. There was that reporter he knew, based in Denver. Walter . . . Walter . . . Mendenhall! I remember how he talked—I think he and Aristotle were young fellas together in West Virginia. But that's all I ever heard about Aristotle's past," lamented Grandpa Joshua.

"Still, it's a place to start," I said, because all this felt alive to me, even if it was a long time ago, and I knew Walter Mendenhall, although he was surely dead by now, would help us, if only I could figure out how.

CHAPTER NINETEEN

Margaret
2014

THIS TIME, IT WASN'T THE GREAT, WHEELING, dancing stars in the sky we put our trust in, but a single star, pink and gray, eight-pointed, and not beautiful, or beautiful only because it had been precious, for whatever reason, to Aristotle.

Our internet search turned up more Mendenhalls than Charlie and I knew what to do with, and after many awkward emails and two mortifying phone calls, just when we were starting to seriously feel like stalkers, we found a Mendenhall family in West Virginia with their own web page and everything: Mendenhall & Sons & Daughters Roofing Company. Right away, I liked them. They'd been around since 1868. They included "& Daughters" in their company name. They specialized in slate and tile, two solid, high-quality materials. I had a good feeling about these Mendenhalls.

"I bet these are *our* Mendenhalls," I said to Charlie, because that's the point we'd gotten to: Aristotle was part of us; he belonged to us and so did his Mendenhalls.

"Yeah," said Charlie, "I bet so, too."

One of these Mendenhalls—Edith, who I assumed was one of the "& Daughters" daughters (or more likely great-great-great granddaughters)—answered our email within three hours, and she not only didn't act like we were totally insane or possible creepers but offered enthusiastically to help us in any way she could.

It turned out that Edith's family, Walter Mendenhall's family, had taken Aristotle in when he had just arrived from Greece and was dirt-poor, still battle-weary from World War I, and totally alone in the world. Which seemed to me like an extremely nice thing to do, but Edith acted like it was nothing special. In fact, she acted like her family members were the ones who got lucky in finding Aristotle, instead of the other way around.

Aristotle Agrippa is still a beloved figure in our family, wrote Edith Mendenhall-Smith. *His loss still haunts us. We know what he tried to do for the miners of Victory, and how hard he worked for justice. I'd call him a family legend, except that sounds so impersonal. He's more like just plain family. How wonderful that you're researching him. We've got a letter from him, one my great-grandfather saved. I'd be happy to scan it and send it to you, if you think it might help.*

Oh, yeah, we thought it just might, and within the hour, there they were, pieces of the past sliding page by page out of the printer in my mom's home office and into our hot little hands. Charlie and I were so excited we were goofy, laughing and jostling to see who could get to the printer first. But as soon as we got a look at the top page, we got quiet because we understood that the letter was a sacred thing. Not in a church way. In a human being way. I sat staring at the page, not even reading, just taking it in, and maybe Charlie was doing the same thing, because after a few seconds, he said, "You know what? We should wait."

"For Grandpa Joshua, you mean," I said.

"Yeah. It only seems right."

Grandpa Joshua had taken Charlie's little brothers to a movie, so we had to wait hours until he got back. It almost killed us. When they finally got home, even before he had quite made it across the threshold of Charlie's house, we each grabbed one of Grandpa Joshua's arms and pulled him through the hallway and the kitchen and out into the backyard.

When we were all outside, I stood there for a moment, with Charlie's yard spread out before me. It was ordinary, littered with balls and toys, Charlie's dad's big old grill hunkered down like a rusty spaceship at one end, the splintery seesaw his mom had built when Charlie and I were little cutting a sharp diagonal against the pearly, streaky, almost-evening sky. The yard looked like it had looked for as long as I could remember, and yet it was different because now it was the place where it had all started, where Grandpa Joshua had sprung the idea of time travel on me like a guy pulling a rabbit out of a hat. It felt right to be there now, to walk over to the picnic table and sit down, with the giant, stern oak tree as witness, and to hand Grandpa Joshua Aristotle's letter.

Aristotle had written it during the miners' strike but before the Canvasburg Massacre, back when it looked like reason and justice would peacefully win out and the four Martinelli kids would all live to adulthood, back before anyone knew just how truly cruel and twisted Elijah Biggs could be. The hope shining in every line of that letter was enough to break your heart. It's funny—you could tell from the writing that Aristotle didn't grow up speaking English, but the broken sentence structure and odd word choices couldn't hide Aristotle's braininess or his sense of humor. The letter had a quirky, honest gracefulness to it. Grandpa Joshua's voice only cracked once, when he read the lines: *Always my boy there watching. My boy the fighter, his strong arm ready to throw. He watch how peace is powerful. This thing, he needs to see.*

Out of the jangly music of the letter, one sentence floated like a gorgeous white bird: *I lived in the virtue of that life and power that took away the occasion of all wars.*

"I remember you telling us about these words before," said Charlie, "or some of them, anyway. Such a cool sentence."

"What do you think it means?" I asked.

"Aristotle said it a lot," said Grandpa Joshua, "whenever we got down and needed our spirits raised. He'd tell us we were taking away the occasion of all wars. Even when I wasn't quite sure what he meant, it made me stand up straighter."

"Can you read that sentence again?" I asked.

Grandpa Joshua did.

Slowly, I said, "So is he saying there's something more powerful than war, something that makes war unnecessary?"

"I think so," said Grandpa Joshua.

"What is it?" I asked.

We all sat, thinking.

"Virtue means goodness, right?" said Charlie, finally. "So maybe that."

I thought about what my dad had said about all the small goodnesses adding up to amazing. I thought about Grandpa Joshua's voice shaking, even after all these years, at the part in the letter where Aristotle talked about Luke. Goodness. Yes, that was right. The kind that connects one person to another person and never goes away.

"Love," I blurted out.

As soon as I said it, I felt embarrassed, not because I

didn't mean it, but because it was just not a word I said that often, even to myself. I could feel Charlie not looking at me. But then Grandpa Joshua was smiling right straight into my eyes.

"Atta girl," he said.

"Hey," said Charlie. "That sentence. It's not how Aristotle talked all the time, is it? All formal and poetic-sounding?"

"No," said Grandpa Joshua. "He was an eloquent man, a gifted speaker, but no, he wasn't fancy like that. Mostly, he sounded more or less like he does in the other parts of the letter."

"It sounds like a quote," said Charlie.

"It does!" I said.

Charlie's eyes met mine for a split second, and then we were off, knocking into each other and tripping over baseballs and grass clumps on a mad dash to the computer. Charlie's mile-long legs got him to the kitchen door first, and before I went in after him, I turned around to call Grandpa Joshua, but then I stopped. He was still sitting where we'd left him, reading Aristotle's letter again in the light of the setting sun.

George Fox, 1624–1691. That's who'd written Aristotle's fancy sentence the first time.

We'd never heard of him, but apparently he'd started something called the Religious Society of Friends, which we'd also never heard of.

"The Religious Society of Friends people are also called Quakers," said Charlie, reading from the computer screen.

We looked at each other, puzzled.

"Oatmeal?" I said.

"Motor oil?" said Charlie.

"Hold on!" I said. "The beard-around-the-edges people!"

"Uh, what?"

"You know! The horse and buggy people. From, like, Pennsylvania."

"Those would be the Amish, genius."

His superior tone of voice demanded an elbow in the ribs, which I dutifully gave him. He elbowed me back, and it was on the edge of becoming a real occasion of war when Charlie's mom called out, "Dinner! Now! Electronic devices of all kinds *off. Now*, people!"

"Am I people, too?" I called back. I hoped so. Mrs. Garrett was making chicken and dumplings. I'd been smelling it for an hour.

"Of course!" called Mrs. Garrett. "Who else would you be?"

* * *

The next day was Saturday. Saturday morning was pancake morning at my house. On this particular morning there were two kinds: caramelized banana with maple syrup and peach with crème fraîche. It definitely did not stink having a pastry chef mom. Charlie agreed and showed up the way he did almost every Saturday morning, but sadly, we were in too much of a hurry to get to the library and research George Fox and the Quakers to give the pancakes the attention they deserved. Still, Charlie managed to gobble a truly disgusting number of them, and I wasn't far behind. We were still chewing when we jumped on our bikes and headed to the Victory Public Library.

Sure, we could've just researched online, but full disclosure (and we didn't exactly go around broadcasting this, not that anyone would've been that surprised, since our nerdiness was a fairly well-established fact): Charlie and I flat-out loved the library. It was the first place we'd ever walked to alone together, without any adults, so maybe we got used to it feeling like an adventure. What I think we loved best about it was the sense of possibility: the sight of all those books just lined up, one after the other after the other, with whole worlds clapped between their covers.

When we found the section with books on Quakerism, we did what we always did: plopped down at the end of the aisle, onto the old, worn, sand-colored library rug, our backs against the wall and with stacks of books on either side of us. More than once, when we were a lot younger, we'd stayed so long that the librarian, Mrs. Goldshine, had found us slumped against each other, fast asleep.

Our only plan—mainly because we couldn't think of anything else to do—was to read about George Fox and his Religious Society of Friends and see where it took us. So we read, and every now and then, we'd library-voice each other bits and pieces of information, anything that seemed useful or just plain interesting.

As far as Charlie and I could tell, most of what George and the Friends believed seemed to stem from one idea: God was everywhere and lived like a light inside every single person. So if a person wanted to hear God, all they had to do was listen to what was right there inside them.

What this also meant, at least to Fox and many other Friends, was that you couldn't justify killing, hurting, or mistreating other people, because they had just as much light in them as you did. So most of the Quakers ended up being pacifists, meaning they refused to fight in wars because they didn't believe in killing other people no matter what.

What I liked best, though, was that "pacifist" didn't mean passive. It wasn't enough to just refuse to hurt people; you had to get out there and *work*, do whatever you could think of to make the world a better place, not just for yourself or people like you, but for everyone. So there was a bunch of Quakers who spent their lives trying to help people, feed them, heal them, give them rights.

"Susan B. Anthony!" I whispered to Charlie, "And Lucretia Mott."

"William Penn, the guy who founded Pennsylvania," whispered Charlie. "Listen to what he said, 'Force may subdue, but love gains, and he that forgives first wins the laurel.'"

There it was again, that word, right there between me and Charlie. *Love.* I tried to will myself not to blush, which is obviously impossible, so I settled for blushing and then feeling really stupid about it.

"Oh yeah. That's right up Aristotle's alley," I said.

And a few minutes later, Charlie said, "The Society of Friends was the first group in the country to officially call for abolishing slavery."

"Yeah, I just read that, too. A lot of the families who worked the Underground Railroad were Quakers," I said. "Like Nathan and Polly Johnson, who helped Frederick Douglass get free."

"Peaceful activism. Fighting injustice without literally fighting. That's total Aristotle. No wonder his motto was from a Quaker guy," said Charlie.

Then we made two big discoveries. Actually, it was kind of nice, how we each got to make one. Charlie's was first. He found it in a book about prominent Quaker families.

"Look!" he almost yelled.

From somewhere nearby, an invisible person hissed, "Shh!"

"Look," he whispered.

He was pointing to something in the book. A name: *Mendenhall.*

"They were Friends!" I said. "That's how he learned all that stuff."

"It says here that the family was part of a big Quaker settlement that did a bunch of good things, including feeding the kids of coal miners in West Virginia when they were starving, and making sure they had medicine."

My discovery came maybe half an hour later. I was reading about how during World War I, Quakers formed a group that didn't go to battle but that worked for the country in other ways: driving ambulances, nursing the injured, and staying in Europe after the war to help people rebuild their towns. And there it was, at the bottom of the page. For a few seconds, I didn't even recognize it because it was so sharp-edged and clear, with bold black and red points: Aristotle's talisman, a symbol of serving your community without using violence.

I'm almost positive I stopped breathing; it's also possible that my heart stopped beating. But as soon as everything clicked back on, I turned the book to face Charlie, who also froze for a moment, then touched the picture with one finger.

"There it is," he whispered.

He scooted over until our shoulders were touching, and we sat like that for a while, staring at the star. Then something happened.

"Do you feel it?" asked Charlie slowly, his voice full of wonderment.

"Maybe," I said. "What do you mean?"

"The tug," said Charlie. "Pieces of the past and pieces of the present pulling toward each other and stitching themselves together."

There was something wonderful about Charlie just then, wonderful and almost spooky, and you know what? As soon as he'd said that strange thing, I *did* feel it.

"Like a quilt?" I said.

"Yeah."

"Can you see what the pieces are making?" I asked, carefully. "The pattern?"

Charlie shook his head.

"But I know what it is," he said, looking up from the book and right at me with intense eyes. "So do you. It's history. Not the past, not the kind that resists. I mean it's the history we're making right now."

I shut the book with a bang and stood up.

"Let's go get the talisman," I said. "And Grandpa Joshua!"

CHAPTER TWENTY

Charlie
2014

WE COULDN'T WAIT TO TELL Grandpa Joshua everything we'd found out, so I called him from the library and blurted, "We know what the talisman is and we'll tell you when we get home."

And I guess he was as impatient as we were, so he said, "How about if I meet you halfway. At The Octagon?"

As Margaret and I rode, I realized that even though it felt like The Octagon had been mine and hers forever, it must mean something special to Grandpa Joshua, too. Back when it was a whole gazebo, it had brought Margaret to him, and it had taken her away. Before long, we were all three kneeling on the smooth old boards staring at Aristotle's talisman in the stark, water-clear afternoon sunlight.

And maybe because I knew now that the star stood

for so much, and I looked at it with new eyes and deeper expectations, I saw something I'd missed: marks in three of the pink points.

"A number?" I whispered. "In the bottom point. A number ten. And a dash."

"And a two," added Margaret right away. "And a seven. Twenty-seven."

"Ten twenty-seven nineteen thirty-eight," said Grandpa Joshua. He was sitting up, not even looking at the square.

"The date of the meeting in the hunting lodge!" Margaret said.

"Aristotle always did like to be precise about things," replied Grandpa Joshua.

"About what, though?" I wondered.

"AA," Margaret said, her eyes on the square. "And the writing on this other point is really hard to read, but I bet it says—"

"TR," said Grandpa Joshua, finally looking at the square again. "Theodore Ratliff. Aristotle brought his old pen to that meeting. It would write on anything. Aristotle and Mr. Ratliff used it to sign Aristotle's talisman."

"And date it," I said, feeling all the pieces of history fall together with a clunk like a drawbridge dropping into place. "Aristotle brought the talisman to commemorate the moment!"

"The moment when his ideals, the Quaker star ideals,

worked," said Margaret, "when words and respect beat out armored cars and guns."

"And don't forget the 'For Luke' on the back," I said.

"He was going to give the star to Luke," said Grandpa Joshua, "to show him how powerful peace can be. Because that's what he'd been trying to show Luke all along. And this would've been the proof. His memento."

"His ideals *did* work!" I shouted, surprised at how angry I felt. "Theodore Ratliff was going to do the right thing! He signed the agreement *and* initialed the star. But then . . ." I pointed to the remaining points, all blank.

"There's no EB. Elijah Biggs never signed the star," Margaret said, bitterly.

"Because of this," said Grandpa Joshua sadly, pointing to the big, brown stain.

"This is Aristotle speaking to Luke, even from beyond the grave," I said, picking up the square. "Telling him that his father wasn't weak or a liar or a murderer. Telling him that peace can be as strong and brave as anything."

"If only he could've gotten his message to Luke," lamented Margaret.

"Arisotle couldn't. But we will!" I cried. "We'll save Lucas Biggs, and we'll save your dad!"

Grandpa Joshua smiled. "We just might," he said.

* * *

I guess Margaret and I should've seen what was coming next, since Judge Biggs had such a long and distinguished history of ignoring evidence. But we didn't. We foolishly thought he'd be as anxious to get Aristotle's message as we were to deliver it. So we ran home and dialed the courthouse.

Of course, a guy like the Honorable Judge Lucas Biggs doesn't answer his own telephone.

We asked the voice on the other end if we could make an appointment to see the judge.

Were we a colleague in the judiciary? wondered the voice.

No, Margaret and I had to admit. We weren't. But we had something really important to tell Judge Biggs.

Were we a municipal, county, state, or federal official?

No. But this was information he'd definitely want to hear.

Were we an attorney?

No. But this had to do with one of his cases.

Were we with the newspaper?

Not exactly. But in addition to affecting one of his cases, the case of John O'Malley, no less, what we had to say was going to change the judge's entire life.

Not *exactly* with the newspaper? Then *exactly* who were we with?

Uh. Actually one of us was John O'Malley's daughter

and the other one was her friend Charlie. Oh. And we also had Charlie's grandfather on standby—he used to be the judge's best friend back when they were thirteen; he was sitting on the bed folding his laundry and listening. And he said—

Click. BZZZZZZZZZ . . .

Grandpa Joshua said we'd have a better chance of cornering the judge if he didn't come with us. So Margaret and I took the Quaker star, hiked downtown, and parked ourselves by the courthouse door.

It wasn't until three hours later, after the sun had set, that the judge came out. Margaret hollered his name.

At first, I thought he was playing a game, which seemed odd, since the guy was nearly ninety and not exactly known for his sense of humor. "Who said that?" demanded Judge Biggs, staring through Margaret and me like we were ghosts.

"Judge Biggs," panted Margaret excitedly. "Look!" She fumbled in her pockets for the star, but she was nervous.

"I have no time to waste," roared Judge Biggs, focusing his eyes on her at last, "on the children of criminals."

Carefully removing his gaze from Margaret and her trembling hands, he strode toward a colossal black car waiting at the curb. I took a deep breath and jumped in his way. And to my horror, the judge looked at me. His eyes searched my face curiously as if I'd just stepped out of a forest to bring him news from a faraway civilization. But abruptly, he changed his mind about hearing my news and turned away.

"If they come near the courthouse again," snarled Judge Biggs to a bailiff hurrying up, "arrest them." And he folded himself up behind the wheel of his black Cadillac and drove off.

"Lucas Biggs," explained Grandpa Joshua when we told him what'd happened, "has been dealing in lies so long that he's lost faith in the power of truth, lost it so long ago that he's forgotten how to see the truth even when it's right in front of him."

"But we'll restore his faith," said Margaret matter-of-factly, smoothing the Quaker star on her knee, "when we show him this."

I reached out, and she handed it to me. "But," I mused, "if Grandpa's right, he won't look until he gets his faith back, and if Margaret's right, he won't get his faith back until he looks!"

"And unfortunately," said Grandpa Joshua ruefully, "I think we're *both* right."

* * *

Margaret had told me how, back in 1938, Grandpa Joshua set off a blasting cap behind the old infirmary to distract everybody while she ran down the hall to spring Aristotle Agrippa. And it sounded like the plan had worked fine, right up to the part where Aristotle refused to have any part of it.

So I devised a plot of my own, along similar lines, to get into the courthouse to see the judge. I convinced myself I'd better not tell Margaret about it, because the last thing she needed was to get in even deeper trouble with Judge Biggs. Plus, in the back of my mind, I knew if I let her in on the plan, there was a good chance she'd say it was a terrible idea and tell me not to do it.

And I wanted to do it.

I hid behind the Victory courthouse in the rain holding a Green Giant smoke bomb left over from the Fourth of July. The bomb was my version of blasting caps. The commotion it caused would allow me to slip in, corner Judge Biggs, and jam that Quaker star in front of his nose for him to see, really see. If I had to tie him to his chair and prop his eyes open with toothpicks, well, I would run right over to Safeway and buy a box.

I went through my soggy matches in about forty seconds without raising so much as a spark, and the rain fell harder every second, and as I eyed the electrical outlet by the back door, I wondered if it would be possible to light the fuse of my smoke bomb by yanking a coat hanger out of the nearest trash can, jamming it into the socket, and using the resulting sparks to light the sopping fuse. I paused briefly to reflect that I'd come to the point in the story where some guy with a square jaw usually mutters, "That's so crazy it just might work," and then, since there wasn't a guy like that in sight, I went ahead and stuck the coat hanger into the socket. Of course, the sparks that spewed out didn't light the sopping fuse any better than my matches had, but I personally got a pretty good jolt, and I blew every fuse in the old-fashioned courthouse, plus I saw a few stars, and maybe a couple of planets.

While pandemonium reigned inside, I shook the constellations out of my brain and staggered upstairs to the judge's office. I found him hunched over in the dim rainy-day light filtering through his window, oblivious to all the noise, scratching away at something on his desk. Hearing me come in, he furtively stuffed whatever it was beneath a law book at his elbow.

When he saw who I was, a smile spread across his face. I understood what Grandpa Joshua meant about that smile. It was yellow, foul, and weary, with a whiff of boredom, a dash of distaste, and a hint of anger, but no trace of humor, and in the middle of it all lurked a colossal empty blank. I felt like a January wind had poured off the side of Mount

Hosta and swirled down the back of my shirt.

"Don't fool yourself into thinking that it makes one iota of difference," he warned me, "that I was once friends with your grandfather."

"Could you just look—" I pleaded, spreading the Quaker star in front of him on his desk.

"I've seen all I need to see," hissed the judge.

"But you don't even know what it is!" I insisted. "It's from your—"

"I've seen all I *ever* need to see!" bellowed Judge Biggs. "Now leave before I have you locked up!"

"Please—"

"Bailiff!" he roared.

I turned to go. I picked up the Quaker star.

But that wasn't all I picked up.

What in the world could possibly embarrass a man like Judge Biggs? I wondered. What would he need to stash under his books when somebody walked into the room like he was a fifth grader hiding a love note?

Why not pilfer it and see?

CHAPTER TWENTY-ONE

Margaret
2014

CHARLIE AND I WERE DOWN but not out. No way. We just needed a little time to regroup and strategize a plan for getting Judge Biggs to listen to us. We tried to think like generals or chess players, although sometimes, I admit, we just had conversations like this one:

Charlie: "I bet if the judge's got a light inside him, like the Quakers say, it's a bare-minimum light, like a microscopic bioluminescent shrimp at the bottom of the ocean."

Me: "A microscopic bioluminescent shrimp that's been swallowed by a giant sea slug at the bottom of the ocean."

Charlie: "A single-celled bioluminescent bacterium stuck to the butt of the bioluminescent shrimp that's been swallowed by a giant sea slug at the bottom of the ocean."

Etc.

And then the *Victory Voice* published my letter, my thank-you note to the town of Victory.

For days after the letter came out in the paper, our phone rang off the hook with nice, hugely embarrassing calls from friends, neighbors, teachers, relatives. My dad even somehow got hold of the letter and used the one short phone call he got that week to say that he loved me harder than rocks and older than stars and bigger than time. After every phone call, my mom either told me she was proud of me or just *looked* it, and even though I was happy that all this was happening, I flat-out couldn't wait for it to be over.

I'm sure it would've been over long before the end of that week, too, except that even our small-town newspaper has an online edition, and the letter went viral. Modestly viral. Very modestly. I wasn't even in the same viral universe as the cranky-faced cat or the flash mob marriage proposal or any of the bazillion cute puppies or hip-hopping toddlers, but the *Voice* did forward me a bunch of emails from folks who had read and liked my letter, some of them from places I'd only ever read about in books, like Prince Edward Island, Canada, and Brooklyn, New York.

Not from Providence, Rhode Island, though. I didn't get an email from there. What I got instead, one Saturday evening when Charlie and I were sitting in my family room playing chess and brainstorming, for the umpteenth time, how to get that talisman in front of Judge Biggs's big, mean face, was a knock on the front door.

It was a woman in a bright blue sweater with bright blue eyes to match and wild dark hair wrangled into a French twist, curls sproinging out all around her face, which happened to be just exactly the kind of hair I'd always wished I had. She was young and tall and smart-looking.

The first thing she said was "I swear I'm not a stalker."

She put up her hand, like a person taking a vow, and laughed a nervous little laugh.

"Oh," I said, "that's good, I guess."

Then she tipped her head to one side, thinking.

"Well, I am a total stranger from out of town who tracked down where you live and came knocking on your door out of the blue, so I guess . . ."

"You kind of are a stalker?"

She laughed again.

My mom's voice came from the kitchen: "Margaret, who is it?"

Then Charlie came up next to me and said, "Margaret, your mom wants to know who it is."

We looked at the woman, who put out her hand for me to shake, which, after just a second's hesitation, I did. Even if she was a stalker, she seemed like a nice one.

"I'm Charlotte," she said. "I read your letter. My, uh, my family used to live around here."

"I'm Margaret," I said, "and this is Charlie."

"Hi," said Charlie. "Wait. Did you say 'Charlotte'?"

"Yes," said Charlotte.

"So?" I said.

Charlie stiffened and flushed. "Uh, nothing. Nope. That name doesn't ring a bell at all. No, sir."

"Weirdo," I muttered, poking him in the ribs.

"Margaret?" called my mother.

"It's Charlotte," I yelled over my shoulder. "She read my letter. Her family used to live around here."

"Well, invite her in, for heaven's sake," yelled my mother. "You're probably letting moths in."

Right on cue, a gray moth floated past Charlotte and through the front door.

In a matter of minutes, Charlotte was sitting in our living room with a cup of coffee and a chunk of my mom's shortbread in front of her, explaining her connection to Victory, which at first seemed like not much of a connection at all, since both she and her mom before her had grown up in Rhode Island, and her father was from Madrid, Spain. Charlotte explained that she had just finished graduate school back east with a degree in ecology. She told us quite a lot about herself, actually, except for one thing.

"Charlotte, why don't you tell us what brought you here?" asked my mother, when Charlotte had stopped for breath. My mom's voice was polite, but she had an expression on her face that I recognized, one that said, *Answering this question is not optional*.

Charlotte's eyes widened for a second, and she said, in a fluttery way, "Oh, that! Ha ha. Yes, you must be thinking, 'Who is this crazy girl coming all the way from Rhode Island?'"

My mother smiled, faintly. "Something like that," she said.

Charlotte's own smile faded, and she sighed.

"Right. Look," she said, leaning forward, "my grandparents were married here in Victory, and my grandmother left before my mother turned a year old. Left her house and her husband and never looked back. She hated this place. My mother never knew her own father, and she never came back to Victory, not once. I swore I never would either. And then I saw your letter, Margaret."

Her eyes when she looked at me were like pieces of summer sky.

"If I were in your situation, I would've been too mad to write a letter like that. I think I would've wanted to do what my grandma did, turn my back on the whole place. But you, you were so bighearted, so thankful."

I wanted to tell her about how it was a matter of simple math: good + good + good + good > BAD. But I didn't want to interrupt.

"And I realized that that was something I wanted to

learn," Charlotte said, "so I started by learning everything I could about you and your family."

Charlotte shook her head, making her curls jump around.

"It was so wrong, what happened to your dad," she said.

"It sure was," I said.

"I am so sorry."

It was strange; she didn't say it the way people usually did, to mean she was sad for us. She said it like something was her fault.

"Why?" said my mother, puzzled. "You haven't done anything wrong."

"Maybe not, but, well—" Charlotte took a deep breath and said, "I came here to face my grandmother's demons, I guess. Or demon. And to help."

"With what?" I asked.

"Freeing your father, of course," said Charlotte, like that should've been obvious.

Charlie and I looked at each other, startled.

"Well, that's very kind of you," began my mother, "but frankly, I don't—"

That's as far as she got before Charlie cut her off by almost shouting, "Margaret and I need to talk to Lucas Biggs, the judge from her father's trial. Talk to him in person."

I stared at him, stunned. How could he blurt that out

in front of a total stranger *and* with my mom sitting right there, my mom who knew nothing about what he and I had been up to? The really strange thing, though, was that as soon as he said it, the air in the room changed until it felt almost like time travel; everything lit up, shimmering, and *full*. Charlotte's eyes flooded with tears, and she pressed her hands to her mouth.

When she took her hands away, she said, "Oh, Charlie. I am either the best person for that job or the very, very worst."

Before I could really register this, my mother was turning to me and Charlie in amazement.

"Judge Biggs?" she said. "Charlie. Margaret. Why on earth?"

Now that Charlie had let the cat out of the bag, I made the split-second decision not to try to stuff it back in.

"We can change his mind," I told her. "I know it."

She reached out and touched my hair. "Oh, honey, if only it were that simple."

"No," I said, impatiently. "It's not just that we think we're such nice kids that we can talk the big, bad judge into releasing Dad. Charlie and I have something real to show Judge Biggs that will make him see things in a new way. I promise you."

"What is it?" asked my mom.

This time Charlie managed to keep silent, thank

goodness. But I wished with all my heart that we could tell her. She definitely deserved to hear the whole story, but I just wasn't ready to tell her about the time travel. She knew about the O'Malley family quirk, of course. My dad had told her long ago, before they'd gotten married, but if she knew I'd gone back on the forswearing, she might be so mad and worried that she'd watch me like a hawk, which would make it way too hard to do what Charlie and I needed to do (whatever that was) to get my dad free.

"I can't tell you right now," I said. "But I need you to trust me."

My mother sat very still for a moment, considering this, and her face was awfully stern, but then she took a deep breath, cupped my cheek in her hand, and smiled.

"Oh my girl," she said, "*that* I can do."

I swore to myself that someday, just as soon as all of this was over, I would tell her everything.

"But Charlotte, what did you mean?" I asked. "When you said that you were either the best person or the worst to get us in to see the judge?"

For a second, Charlotte seemed to deflate. Then she gathered herself, ran her hand over her messy, beautiful hair, and started to talk.

"My grandmother took her baby and left her husband because he wasn't the man she thought he was. I guess he put on a good act there for a while, but he turned out to be rotten. So rotten that when she left him, she dropped his last name like a dirty rag and left it behind, too."

Even though I had no idea of what was coming next, a shiver went up my spine.

"That name was Biggs," said Charlotte. "Judge Lucas Biggs is my grandfather."

That night, the moon was nowhere in sight, and the stars over The Octagon looked like shoals of fish, so silver, densely packed, and swirling. Charlie and I lay on our backs, taking in the sky, and talking about what we—a "we" that now included not just me, Charlie, and Grandpa Joshua, but Charlotte, too—should do next.

"He might not agree to see her," I said, deciding to go ahead and set the worst possibility out there right away. "I mean, he never tried to see her grandmother or her mother or her, not in all those years."

"But like Charlotte said, he did send her birthday cards, every year," said Charlie.

"That she had to dig out of the trash because her mom threw them away before she could look at them."

"Well, she still dug them out," Charlie said. "And even when she moved to a new house, even when she went away to college, he found out her address and kept on sending her cards. Birthday cards, Christmas cards, graduation cards."

"I don't remember that she said anything about graduation cards, but yeah. I guess he was—being nice? I mean, they were cards, right? Not letter bombs."

Charlie scoffed, "Cards signed *Lucas Biggs*. No 'love,' no 'Grandpa', no gift certificate to the ice-cream shop."

I sat up and stared at Charlie.

"What? How would you know that? Charlotte didn't say how they were signed."

Charlie winced. "Oh man."

He told me all about his plot to create a diversion and break into Judge Biggs's office. Even in the midst of being furious that he hadn't bothered to include me in it or even tell me about it afterward, I couldn't help but be impressed that his plan had worked.

"I'm sorry," he said. "I'm pretty sure attempting to detonate an explosive device outside a state building and breaking into a judge's office are major criminal offenses. I still don't know why the judge didn't turn me in. I guess he just wanted to get rid of me. But I thought it would be better if you stayed out of it, better for you *and* for your mom and dad."

Maybe because he had a point or because he truly did sound sorry or because I'm just really bad at being mad at Charlie, I decided to forgive him.

"All right," I said, "but I still don't see how you know how Judge Biggs signs his birthday cards."

"Graduation, actually grad school graduation," said Charlie. "Which brings me to the possible mail tampering part of my story. On Judge Biggs's desk, I found a graduation card to Charlotte signed by the judge and an envelope with her address. So—"

"You *stole* it?"

"Uh, yeah. I mailed it, though! But not before I'd addressed my own envelope and sent her a copy of your letter, and a couple of other articles about the trial, along with a note that just said 'FYI.' I didn't sign it or anything. Honestly, I didn't even know who she was to Judge Biggs, but I figured if there was anybody out there in the world who cared about him, they might want to know what he's been up to."

"Wow," I said. "Well, thanks for committing all those federal offenses on my behalf."

"No problem," said Charlie. "But even though right now, Charlotte's our best bet, even if she can get us into his office, that doesn't mean he'll look at the Quaker star."

"I was just thinking the same thing. He might look at it if we stick it in front of his face, but that doesn't mean he'll *see* it. Or that he'll give a monkey's rear end what we have to say about it."

We fell silent, the immense night shining around us.

Finally, Charlie said, "We need a hook, one really good line."

"What do you mean?"

"You saw the judge back in the parking lot the other day. He can slam the door in someone's face in record time, even when there's no door in sight. Even if Charlotte gets his attention, we won't have it for long before he goes into shutdown mode. We need a good first line, one that grabs him so hard, he has to keep listening."

"How about: your dad wasn't a coward, you giant bonehead?"

"Okay, but maybe we should give it a little more thought," said Charlie, dryly.

So we did. We stayed so quiet and stared at those stars for so long that it was like The Octagon broke loose from the field, from everything familiar, and became a raft on a huge black ocean, and we were drifting on its surface, cut off from everything and everyone, starlight pouring down.

And that's when I decided to do it. No, that's wrong. I didn't decide. I *believed*. I *knew*. Without knowing why or caring why, I knew I had to do it, and before I fully realized that I had begun, I had begun.

October 28, 1938; October 28, 1938; October 28, 1938. It was the date when I'd left the past and come back, the date of Aristotle's hanging, the date that marked the end of the life of Luke Agrippa and the beginning of the long, twisted journey of Lucas Biggs.

Everything was the same as the first time I'd traveled,

except familiar. I floated inside the in-between space, the glowing, peaceful, endlessly long corridor between times, music in my ears, and all around me, the portals blinking open and shut, beckoning. But then I did something I hadn't done the last time. I began to think more carefully and clearly than I'd ever thought before, to *contemplate*.

The universe is big, I thought. *Time is long. Passing through is hard.*

I thought this, and I understood how I had been able to do it, the only thing that had made me be able to stand it. It wasn't that I was gifted or clever or brave. Those things by themselves would never have been enough. It was just this: *I wasn't alone.* Even when I was by myself, moving through time, I wasn't alone. There was Joshua Garrett on one end and Charlie Garrett on the other. There was my mother at home and my father who could be locked away miles from me and still be with me all the same.

Then I thought about what it would be like to travel through all that time the long way around, along all its loops and turns, experiencing every bit of it, more than seventy years' worth of days, one after the other, *alone*. Alone and believing you'd been abandoned by the person you'd loved most in all the world. I thought about this and right there, in that peaceful place, sadness blew through me like a desolate wind, the same sadness that had been blowing through Lucas Bigg's soul since October 28, 1938.

October 28, 1938. The portal bloomed open before me. It was right there, an arm's length away, waiting. I moved toward it.

Then I did what I was meant to do all along. I stepped back. I went home to the people I loved.

When I got there, one of those people was yelling at the top of his lungs and shaking me by the shoulders until my teeth rattled, at least until he dropped me, with a yelp like he'd just grabbed an electric fence. My head hit the boards of The Octagon with a thunk, but I hardly noticed.

"Charlie! Listen! I have it! The hook! Our opening line!"

"Listen? Listen? Are you insane?"

Charlie was so mad sparks were practically flying off him.

"You don't understand—" I began.

"You were going to *travel*? Without telling me? And don't even deny it. You were in that weird trance like before. I *saw* you! Then, when I touched you, there was this jolt. Jolts like that just don't happen, Margaret!"

I sat up and rubbed the back of my head.

"Would you shut up and listen?" I said.

Charlie shut up, but he was still furious. If he had been a slightly different kind of person, he might've hit me or at least called me a really mean name.

"It wasn't that Luke thought his father was a coward," I said.

Charlie shook his head in confusion.

"What?"

"That's what we thought all along, right? And, sure, Luke probably did think that, and he didn't like it, but that wasn't his main problem. That's not what turned him into Lucas Biggs."

Charlie's breathing slowed down, and he looked down at the boards of The Octagon with his thinking face on, the one I'd seen more times than I could count.

"I wasn't going to travel," I said, softly. "I just needed to go a little way in order to understand the real message of the Quaker star. To see. To look down time and really understand it. It was all part of figuring out how to save Lucas Biggs. In the here and now. With you."

Charlie's eyes met mine and held. After a couple of seconds, he gave a very small nod.

"So if it wasn't that he was ashamed of Aristotle because he thought he was a coward, what was it? What turned him into Lucas Biggs?" he asked.

It was so simple. Why hadn't we seen it before? But I knew why. Charlie and I hadn't spent one second of our lives without parents who loved us. We lived inside that love the way we lived inside our own bodies, without thinking about it, and definitely without thinking what it would be like to live without it.

"He thought his dad had left him," I said. "And not just once. Twice! First by trying to get Ratliff to help him run away, then, when that didn't work, by killing himself. He thought his dad cared about him so little that he could just ditch him and leave."

Charlie pulled in his eyebrows again, pondering.

"So the message of the Quaker star isn't 'I really was brave and the peaceful way really was going to win out in the end'?" said Charlie.

"Maybe that was the message to Luke back then, but the message to him now is: 'I was coming back to you all along.'"

CHAPTER TWENTY-TWO

Charlie
2014

WHEN MARGARET TOLD GRANDPA JOSHUA that the Quaker star was Aristotle's way of saying he never meant to leave Luke, his face slowly lit up.

"You're right," he said. "I only heard the things Luke said about his dad being a coward and a loser. I never listened to what he *didn't* say, that he thought Aristotle had *chosen* to abandon him. I—" He stopped. His eyes widened at the sight of something behind Margaret and me. "You're her!" he exclaimed.

We spun around to see Charlotte walking toward us.

"I only saw her once, when I was home for a visit, but you are the spitting image of your grandmother," Grandpa Joshua went on.

Charlotte laughed.

"Grandpa Josh, this is Charlotte. We told you about

her," put in Margaret.

"Those blue eyes and that dancing hair," said Grandpa Joshua.

"Everybody comments on it," Charlotte replied. "But my grandmother was much more beautiful. Still is, as a matter of fact." She frowned. "Do you think it's a good thing, how much I look like her? Do you think it'll help?"

"She was walking down the street with Luke that day," remembered Grandpa Joshua. "It must've been right after they met. He looked at her like there was no one else in the world."

"There was, though," said Charlotte. "Elijah Biggs and his whole crooked corporation, expecting Lucas Biggs to do their dirty work without batting an eye. My grandmother ended up hating him for it."

"So it could go either way, that face of yours. It could melt his heart," said Grandpa Joshua.

"Or turn it to stone," finished Margaret.

"But we have to try," I said.

"So what we'll do," Charlotte went on, "is march into his office and tell the secretary who I am and demand to see him. And if that doesn't work, I'll wait till he comes out and pounce. I'm a pretty good pouncer."

But Grandpa Joshua shook his head.

"What's wrong?" I asked.

"Aristotle's message has to reach a place buried so deep

in Luke's soul, he's forgotten it exists," said Grandpa Joshua.

"How can we make him remember?" Margaret asked.

"You can't make him. He has to *want* to remember," said Grandpa Joshua. "He has to come to you."

"Lucas Biggs doesn't *want* anything," I said, "except to be left alone."

"He wants to see his granddaughter," Margaret reminded us. "Call him, Charlotte," she urged. "Ask him to meet you, away from the courthouse and the Victory Corporation."

"I may know a place," added Grandpa Joshua, staring distantly toward the edge of town.

"Just tell me where," said Charlotte, pulling out her cell phone.

But something about the plan bothered me. I guess Grandpa Joshua could see it in my face. "What's wrong, Charlie?" he asked.

"It's just—what if he *doesn't* come? What if he wants to see Charlotte, but not enough? He's been alone for so long. What if he just wants to keep going the way he always has?"

"But there are the birthday cards he sent me," said Charlotte.

"There's also the way he looked at you the other day, Charlie," Margaret reminded me. "For like two seconds there, he seemed almost human. I bet it was because you look so much like his old friend Josh."

"That didn't buy me much slack in his office," I reminded her.

"You might be right, Charlie," said Grandpa Joshua. "Even if the real Luke Agrippa is still in there somewhere, Lucas Biggs might figure change is too hard. We're old, the judge and I. Sometimes being old can make you want to give yourself one last chance to be better, but sometimes it can make you bone-deep scared of anything new. So he might not come. But you know what?"

"What?" we all three asked.

What Grandpa Joshua said next wasn't exactly comforting, but not one of us could deny it. "If he doesn't show up, he was never going to listen to his father's message, not in this lifetime. If he doesn't come, none of this was ever going to work anyway."

CHAPTER TWENTY-THREE

Margaret
2014

THE PLACE GRANDPA JOSHUA chose for the meeting with Lucas Biggs was a park on the edge of town, a rectangle of green and trees, redwood picnic tables and benches, a swing set, a few barbecue grills and volleyball nets, everything painted and kept up, but nothing fancy.

Charlie and I had been there when we were smaller, had played hide-and-seek among those very trees, without having any idea of what used to be there. How could we? There was no bronze statue, no historical marker commemorating the four Martinelli children's beautiful black eyes or Preston Garrett's fingers flying over a piano keyboard. No one ever took an educational field trip there to hear a guide tell the story of bullets tearing apart the lives of innocents or of a man who wouldn't stop talking about fair play and peace.

But as I walked across the grass with Grandpa Joshua and Charlie, it occurred to me that someone somewhere had cared enough to make sure it hadn't been paved over, turned into a strip mall or a parking lot. Someone had planted trees.

Canvasburg.

Canvasburg, now full of kids' games and family cookouts, cupcake icing melting in the sun; some of the adults banging around a volleyball with the kids; some of them sitting at picnic tables or under trees, talking, with babies against their shoulders or with little ones asleep in their laps. A safe place. A family place. Maybe this was okay after all. Maybe it was even a kind of justice.

We didn't hide. The place was so busy that we didn't have to. Grandpa Joshua, Charlie, and I were just another family under a tree, soaking up the sound of laughter and the late-spring sun. Charlotte sat at a picnic table by herself, reading a book, waiting for Lucas Biggs. We were all waiting for him, with our hearts in our throats, waiting for Lucas Biggs, inside whom there was at least a tiny bit of Luke Agrippa, shining like a light, or so we hoped.

Charlotte had told him five o'clock. He hadn't said yes or no or much of anything at all. Five o'clock came and went. So did 5:10. Then 5:15 crept up and slipped past. By 5:30, Charlie, Grandpa Joshua, and I had given up on our forced conversation. By 5:40, I was fighting back tears.

Then, at 5:41, there he was, wearing a suit and tie in the evening, making his way across the grass. He moved slowly but steadily, with long strides, and for a second, I could glimpse the athlete he used to be. I saw Charlotte stand up. I saw him walk toward her and stop, a few feet away. I started to walk, too, the quilt square in my hand, but Grandpa Joshua caught me gently by the elbow, pulling me back.

"Wait," he said. "Let's give them a little more time."

They didn't hug, but I saw Judge Biggs lift his hand toward Charlotte's hair, like he was thinking about touching it, and then he changed his mind. They talked.

"Now," said Grandpa Joshua.

I walked quickly across the grass, keeping Charlotte between me and the judge, and at the last second, I stepped out from behind her, holding the Quaker star. I saw Judge Biggs's face begin to go from open to shut, but before he could actually slam the door and hang a Closed sign in the window, I was stretching out my arm, handing him the cloth square.

"Your father was always going to come back to you," I said, as fast as I could get the words out.

Lucas Biggs took a step back, and my heart sank, but then he reached out his broad hand, the hand that had thrown a football almost to the moon, that had pounded the gavel to quiet the courtroom at my father's trial, and he took the Quaker star.

Then Charlie was handing him my dad's magnifying glass, and the two of us were talking at once, pointing out the star shape, the initials, the date.

"'For Luke,'" read the judge. Then again, "'For Luke.'"

A change came over Lucas Biggs. He crumpled, got smaller inside his gray business suit, and then Charlotte moved so that she was next to him, her arm steadying him, leading him to the picnic bench, where he sat down, put his father's talisman on the table in front of him, and stared at it, his fingers pressing down the four corners so he could see the whole thing.

When he looked up, it wasn't at me or at his granddaughter, but at Grandpa Joshua.

"Josh?" he said. "It's true?"

"It's true, Luke," said Grandpa Joshua. "He loved you. Even when he was up in that hunting lodge trying to make history and change the world, he was thinking mostly about you and what he'd bring back to you."

Luke stared back down at the Quaker star, and to my amazement, there was the ghost of a smile on his face, not a sneer or a smirk, but a real smile.

"My mother and I made this. I must've been about four. The big, zigzag stitches in this corner are mine. It was going to be a whole quilt for my father, but my mother died before we could finish."

Luke folded his hands into two fists, set them down on top of the square, and rested his forehead against them. He sat like that, his shoulders shaking with silent sobs, as kids ran past and the smell of barbecue filled the air. Grandpa Joshua, Charlotte, Charlie, and I stood by, not talking, not comforting him or even looking at him, just staying, for as long as it took.

CHAPTER TWENTY-FOUR

Josh
2014

BRIDEY'S HOUSE WAS NOTHING but a ruin. The walls had fallen outward and the roof had fallen inward and her garden had blown, seed by seed, through its fence and taken root where her kitchen used to be. Pumpkins had snaked through the plumbing and spread their leaves in her sink. Carrots had sprouted among the soles of decaying shoes in what was left of her closet. Pea vines had washed over her back porch like a green tide.

Visiting was Margaret's idea. I wasn't so sure. I knew the place would be a wreck, and maybe a little sad. But Margaret said, "I'm sure Aunt Bridey would be delighted to have us."

I thought back to the very strange day when Bridey had told me that friendship stands the test of time, and I figured I owed her a chance to say, "I told you so," so I agreed to go.

Up the mountain we hiked, two happy families: My grandson Charlie and his mom and dad and brothers and sister. And Margaret and her mother and her newly freed father. The kids swarmed all over everything, looking for treasure—a rotted wooden drawer full of silverware, the spoons still shiny under the tarnish. The translucent golden knobs of an antique radio. A small safe that nobody would ever open, though I somehow knew that inside it lay, safe and dry, an ancient picture of a Confederate Army lieutenant. Margaret had been right. Bridey, wherever she happened to be, was surely thrilled at this spectacle.

I gazed over my shoulder at the peak of Mount Hosta. Two days before, I'd visited it with Lucas Biggs. Not a bad day's hike for two old men. We didn't talk about old times, because they were too far gone. But he did tell me that since he'd vacated John O'Malley's sentence and overturned the guilty verdict, he'd decided to go ahead and finish the job. He'd called the governor and alerted him to the piles of evidence that'd gone unexamined in that trial.

Which meant that Victory Fuels was on the run. Their crimes would come to light. Their hydrofracking plans were wrecked. And to top it all off, Judge Biggs's granddaughter Charlotte, the environmentalist, was busy starting her own company, which, among other things, might build a few windmills to catch that wind blowing off the mountain all day and night. As long as she could figure out how to do it without clonking too many birds on the head.

I had a thousand things to say to Luke, too, but when we got to the top of Mount Hosta and saw the world spread out below us, looking not much different than it had when we were thirteen, the thought of all the things we'd done and all the things we'd left undone was too much. I couldn't speak.

"Our grandchildren will do better than we did," declared Luke, and I heard something in his voice I hadn't heard in seventy-six years: hope. I felt it, too, and I remembered everything I ever loved about Luke Agrippa.

I found my voice and said, "I never stopped being your friend."

"Thank you," said Luke. "Thank you so much, Josh."

We stood quietly for a bit, and I gave him his father's old fountain pen. "I thought you'd like to have it," I said.

"I would, very much," he'd replied with a faint smile on his face, and tucked it into his pocket as we turned for home.

"John!" I called to Margaret's father, who was standing near the edge of Aunt Bridey's old orchard gazing at the horizon, wondering how he would put his life back together. Even if he was worried, I wasn't. I knew he'd think of something. He was an O'Malley. "Let me show you something," I said. "A little secret of your aunt Bridey's."

"She had a lot of them, didn't she?" asked John, his green eyes twinkling behind his glasses.

"This one you're going to like," I replied, rummaging through the vines on the face of the cliff for the entrance to her old dugout pantry. Inside, sure enough, on a wooden shelf that hadn't crumbled yet, there was one bottle. Aunt Bridey's Honey Brook Nectar. I brought it out into the sunlight, offered John O'Malley a seat on the nearest boulder, uncorked the bottle (the cork was a little stiff, but I had all the time in the world), and took a nip. "Here's to the past," I said, offering him the bottle. He took it.

After a thoughtful silence, I worked up the nerve to ask, "Margaret told you the whole story?"

"That she did," John O'Malley replied softly.

"And?" I prodded.

"I wasn't a bit happy," he declared, "although I *was* very proud."

"You know," I ventured after another silence, "it's true that history resists, and it's true that the present is the best place to make things happen. And *maybe*, if Margaret hadn't traveled to 1938, she somehow would've ended up with the Quaker star anyway, and we'd all be right here just the way we are. But . . ."

"Maybe not?" said John O'Malley. "Are you saying that maybe history has a lot to keep track of, a lot bigger things than a little, faded scrap of cloth? Are you saying that maybe sometimes, when history's not paying attention, things slip through? Are you saying the time travel worked?"

"I'm not saying it," I said, with a grin, "and I'm not *not* saying it. But if I *were* saying it, I sure wouldn't say it to Margaret or Charlie."

John laughed, took another swig of the Honey Brook Nectar, and said, "I think not saying it is an excellent idea."

Scrambling through Bridey's spectacular, fallen-down old life, laughing like kids, just kids, kids who hadn't been through more of history than many old men nearing ninety, my tall grandson and his friend Margaret O'Malley made their way toward us.

Margaret's hair was as red and her eyes were as green as they'd been on the day I first met her, back when I was thirteen and she was, too. But she'd been to the optometrist since her dad had been freed, so now she wore glasses. Not too thick, not yet, though I knew they would look like the windows of an armored car before many years passed. That was how it was bound to play out. Those glorious eyes were changing, becoming weaker. Soon they'd be no more special than anybody else's, and in some ways, Margaret herself was becoming just like anybody else, though not completely, because the knowledge living inside her of time and history was a secret only a handful of humans has ever possessed.

Crossing the ruins of the garden, Charlie tripped on

a cucumber vine and crashed into Margaret, and as soon as he got himself steady again, she shoved him down in a patch of brand-new tomatoes, laughing, laughing, laughing, laughing.

"Not to dispute the importance of your family quirk," I told John O'Malley, with a nod toward the two of them, "but sometimes you don't need to be a time traveler to see the future."

CHAPTER TWENTY-FIVE

Margaret
2014

I WON'T SAY THAT I DON'T THINK about the bad things now and then. I've been woken up by the sight of Theodore Ratliff's dead, oyster-wet eyes and by the sound of Judge Biggs's voice sentencing my father to death. I've almost fallen off my bike at the sudden memory of Elijah Biggs, his face swollen with hate, bringing that cane down on Aristotle's skull. And maybe all my life, I'll imagine a sight I never saw but that visits me anyway: Aristotle's poor, battered body swinging from a beam.

But mostly what I think about is all the different ways of being brave.

Aristotle was brave by fighting on his own terms, without bullets or bloodshed. Grandpa Joshua was brave by having faith in Luke, decade after decade, a lifetime's worth of faith, no matter what. My dad was brave by standing up to the Victory Corporation. Charlie was brave by being my friend, by staying, like it was no big deal, through death sentences and smoke bombs and time travel and by taking enormous risks to help me. My mom was brave by serving coffee and cookies to our kind neighbors, even when her heart was breaking. Maybe I was even brave, too, although what might've looked like bravery from the outside was just me loving my dad, same as always.

But on the way back down the mountain, after a day at Aunt Bridey's vine-choked wreck of a house, a day that was possibly the most perfect day in history, I did what felt like the bravest thing I'd ever done, and maybe this sounds weird, but right before I did it, I thought about Lucas Biggs. Because he was brave, too, brave enough to change his life. Maybe there in the park that used to be Canvasburg, when he reached out and took the Quaker star, he felt what I felt as I walked down Mount Hosta with all my favorite people: that sure, the past matters—but the present? The present is here and here and here, a sky full of light, a path under your feet, your hair lifted by wind, the smell of flowers, green grass, red rocks, all of it tumbling toward summer, and all of it yours. All you have to do is set fear aside and stretch out your hand.

Lucas Biggs stretched out his hand. So did I.

I stretched it out, grabbed Charlie's, and held it. He held mine, too, right there in the one now, the spot where we stood, and the road went onward, onward, onward all the way home.

Acknowledgments

Heartfelt thanks to the following people:

our beloved agent, Jennifer Carlson, who told us to go for it with so much enthusiasm that we really couldn't say no;

our editor, Kari Sutherland, who always understood, even when we didn't, and put us through the wringer in the best possible way;

everyone at HarperCollins Children's Books;

Dan Fertel, Isaac Fertel, Annabel Teague, Kristina de los Santos, and everyone else who read *Lucas Biggs* in its early stages and so graciously gave us their thoughts;

the Ballotta Garman family and all the good people at Wilmington Friends School;

Finn and Huxley, loyal and true, who had us wondering how we wrote all those years without dogs at our feet (or on our laps);

our children, Charles and Annabel Teague, who make

us sharper and kinder, better people and better writers, and who are just really great to hang out with.

And finally, David is grateful for Marisa, and Marisa is grateful for David. Writing a book with your best friend—life doesn't get much sweeter than that.